Donald MacKenzie and The Murder Room

››› This title is part of The Murder Room, our series dedicated to making available out-of-print or hard-to-find titles by classic crime writers.

Crime fiction has always held up a mirror to society. The Victorians were fascinated by sensational murder and the emerging science of detection; now we are obsessed with the forensic detail of violent death. And no other genre has so captivated and enthralled readers.

Vast troves of classic crime writing have for a long time been unavailable to all but the most dedicated frequenters of second-hand bookshops. The advent of digital publishing means that we are now able to bring you the backlists of a huge range of titles by classic and contemporary crime writers, some of which have been out of print for decades.

From the genteel amateur private eyes of the Golden Age and the femmes fatales of pulp fiction, to the morally ambiguous hard-boiled detectives of mid twentieth-century America and their descendants who walk our twenty-first century streets, The Murder Room has it all. ›››

The Murder Room

Where Criminal Minds Meet

themurderroom.com

Donald MacKenzie 1908–1994

Donald MacKenzie was born in Ontario, Canada, and educated in England, Canada and Switzerland. For twenty-five years MacKenzie lived by crime in many countries. 'I went to jail,' he wrote, 'if not with depressing regularity, too often for my liking.' His last sentences were five years in the United States and three years in England, running consecutively. He began writing and selling stories when in American jail. 'I try to do exactly as I like as often as possible and I don't think I'm either psychopathic, a wayward boy, a problem of our time, a charming rogue. Or ever was.'

He had a wife, Estrela, and a daughter, and they divided their time between England, Portugal, Spain and Austria.

By Donald MacKenzie

Henry Chalice
Salute from a Dead Man (1966)
Death is a Friend (1967)
Sleep is for the Rich (1971)

John Raven
Zaleski's Percentage (1974)
Raven in Flight (1976)
Raven and the Ratcatcher (1976)
Raven and the Kamikaze (1977)
Raven After Dark (1979)
Raven Settles a Score (1979)
Raven and the Paperhangers (1980)
Raven's Revenge (1982)
Raven's Longest Night (1983)
Raven's Shadow (1984)
Nobody Here By That Name (1986)
A Savage State of Grace (1988)
By Any Illegal Means (1989)
Loose Cannon (1994)
The Eyes of the Goat (1992)
The Sixth Deadly Sin (1993)

Standalone novels
Nowhere to Go (1956)
The Juryman (1957)
The Scent of Danger (1958)
Dangerous Silence (1960)
Knife Edge (1961)
The Genial Stranger (1962)
Double Exposure (1963)
The Lonely Side of the River (1964)
Cool Sleeps Balaban (1964)
Dead Straight (1968)
Three Minus Two (1968)
Night Boat from Puerto Vedra (1970)
The Kyle Contract (1971)
Postscript to a Dead Letter (1973)
The Spreewald Collection (1975)
Deep, Dark and Dead (1978)
The Last of the Boatriders (1981)

Postscript to a Dead Letter

Donald MacKenzie

An Orion book

This edition published by
The Orion Publishing Group Ltd
Orion House
5 Upper St Martin's Lane
London WC2H 9EA

An Hachette UK company
A CIP catalogue record for this book is available from the British Library

ISBN 978 1 4719 0585 8

www.orionbooks.co.uk

People in France have forgotten what the press there
lled L'Affaire Brown. Nevertheless it is Phoebe and
dnor Brown who are responsible for the story that
arted on a highway outside Paris and ended at the
ine Assizes.

Six people, four men and two women, were tried for
urder, abduction, conspiracy and illegal possession of
roin. Their names are Pierre Pelazzi, Commandant
illes Kerambrun, Salvatore Hollier, Guillaume
hmidt, Claire de Pornic and Anne Forbin. A dealer in
rios, a retired officer of the Armee de l'Air, two agents
the C.R.S., the Corps Republicain de Securite, an
nployee of the French Foreign Ministry and the widow
a professional gambler.

All six were sentenced to *reclusion criminelle a per-
tuite,* life-imprisonment.

They were the patsys. Behind them was a ring that
cluded agents of S.D.E.C.E., the Police Judiciaire, a
ovincial prefect and a Marseilles banker. Of these, two
signed and one committed suicide. Pressure from
ove buried the rest of the conspiracy. For as Maitre
sini says, as well try to puncture a balloon with a
ather as get the Union Corse into Court. So the real
iminals, the Capus of the Brotherhood, are sipping
stis on the Cannebiere, arranging shipments of
roin as if it were so much currypowder. What follows

is the only indictment they will ever have to face.
Savai'i. Western Samoa.

N.20 runs as straight as a plumbline at that point. The poplars on each side were naked in the grey November afternoon. Most of the traffic was heading for Paris, the cars loaded down with children and the paraphernalia of the French weekend excursion. It was Sunday so there were no trucks to contend with. Nevertheless I kept the rented Renault in the slow lane. The newscasts promised an imminent snowfall and the cut-and-thrust battle to be home before dark was already on.

My mind was on the man I had just left. By the time he was twenty-eight, Jean-Paul Texier had directed five movies in France. Any one of them would have made his reputation. He undertook the pilgrimage to Hollywood and accepted the accolade. Over the next few years he was responsible for a number of pictures that drew raves in the arthouses and bombed on the circuits. At forty-two, Texier returned to France with his charm and intelligence somehow unimpaired.

I make a living writing about people like Jean-Paul for the London *Post*. It's a daily that carries what's called a Profile Page in the weekly magazine-section. I make my own choice of subject and the field is wide. I've interviewed statesmen, scientists, writers, bank-robbers and jump-jockeys. I look for two qualifications – the subject must be European and he has to be outstanding in his field. A year after it started, the Profile Page was fooling everyone in the building, including me. Periodicals from Iceland to Japan were picking up our material and a constant stream of fan-mail was coming in. Baxter, my boss, was sufficiently impressed to give me a larger room and a fulltime research-assistant called Misty Farrell. 'Research-assistant' is an inadequate way of describing the tiny brunette who can think faster in three languages than most people can in one. Without Misty the whole project would have fallen apart.

There was no radio in the car, nothing to do after settling with Texier but drive with one eye on the traffic that was barrelling by. The copy on Jean-Paul put me two weeks ahead of schedule and I was in no hurry to get back to London. I've been renting a two-room apartment in Chelsea for the last few years but it's a pad, not a home. Most of the time, I'm round at Misty's place. But this was Paris and Ilinka was expecting me for dinner.

It was getting on for four o'clock as I drove through Chapelle-Noisy, a shuttered deserted place with the defeated appearance of a French village on a winter afternoon. I was halfway across the central square when I noticed a police-wagon parked behind some poplars. I put my foot firmly on the brake-pedal. Neither guile nor bribery will get you off the hook with the French traffic-police. I was out of town but still doing a modest thirty miles an hour when a red mini showed up on the grass shoulder ahead. I trod on the brake again. They tell you never to stop for hitch-hikers, especially if there's a goodlooking chick in evidence. It's the sort of advice I rarely seem to take. I walked back to the small stalled car. The hood was up, the girl bent over looking into the motor. She straightened up as I neared, pushing blonde-streaked hair out of her eyes. She was about five feet eight and wearing a tan polo coat. The left sleeve was oil-streaked where she'd been playing around with the works. I learned my French the hard way, three nights a week at the Berlitz School of Languages. The result is fair if you're charitable about the syntax. I flashed a smile to give her confidence.

'Bonjour, Mademoiselle. Il y a des problemes?'

Texier's country place is in the Bois de Verrieres. He keeps a few horses there. I'd driven down for lunch dressed in corduroy slacks and a heavy sweater. Both had picked up a fair amount of straw on the tour through the stables and there was dung on my shoes. The girl took a closer look at me.

'Do you speak English?' Her accent was gently Southern, her eyes almost violet.

'I certainly do,' I said. 'What seems to be the trouble?'

She hesitated for a moment. I put her nervousness down to the fact that she too had heard stories, the ones about not accepting help from strangers. Except that she wasn't alone. A man was sitting on the back seat of the mini. I could see the upper half of his body, a thin face, hair a good deal shorter than mine and heavy spectacles. The girl stepped across my line of vision.

'I can't imagine what's wrong. The motor started missing a few miles back. We just about managed to crawl on to the shoulder then it died completely.'

I walked round to the door on the driver's side. The fuel-gauge showed the tank to be nearly full. The man in the back watched me warily without speaking. I came round the front again and yanked off one of the spark-leads.

'Hit the motor!' I called. The guy made no move.

'He doesn't speak English,' the girl said. 'I'll get it.'

She was wearing no wedding-ring. I figured him as her boyfriend. She stationed herself behind the wheel and switched on the starter. A spark bounced off the cylinder-head. I clipped the lead back and tried the other sparkplugs. All functioned.

'Hit it again,' I said. 'Keep your foot down. The motor might be flooded.'

She stared out as the motor churned uselessly. The sound of the battery told me that it was dying. I dropped the hood and wiped my hands.

'I'm out of ideas. You need a mechanic. There's a gas-station a couple of miles up the highway. You want me to send someone out?'

She left the car and hurried towards me, brushing her hair away with the same quick gesture. She looked from the stream of traffic to the gathering darkness in the fields beyond.

'That would take too long. We *have* to be in Paris.'

It wasn't a direct request but I understood. 'No problem,' I said, indicating the Renault. 'Tell your friend to jump in.'

Once out of the car, he was taller than I expected, wearing a red-and-grey mackinaw over a shirt without a tie. He threw a blue canvas bag on the rear seat and climbed in after it. The girl dropped in beside me. She'd left the mini unlocked and without lights but that was her business. I waited, indicators flashing, for an opportunity to ease back on to the highway.

'I'm making for the Place des Vosges – any good to you?'

She shook her head quickly. 'I guess not, thanks. If you'd just let us off at the first Metro station . . .'

Her fingers were working all the time, I noticed. The only jewellery she wore was an old-fashioned silver watch on a thin leather strap. I couldn't make up my mind about their relationship. They were both on edge, unwilling to speak to one another. A lover's quarrel, I decided. A cortege of police-cars bore down on us, coming from the opposite direction. The noise of the double-noted sirens was deafening. The outriders on motorcycles looked like spacemen in their masked helmets and black leather coats. They rode the dividing strip, waving traffic over as they came. The cars in front of me jammed into the slower lanes, scattered by the flying phalanx. A DS Safari swerved, forcing me up on the grass shoulder. The front wheel of the Renault ploughed into the soft earth. Mud spattered the windshield. I hung on desperately, hearing the blaring horns behind. The car shuddered then righted itself. I swallowed hard, realising that a few more inches and the Renault would have been travelling on its side. The guy behind me had whipped off his spectacles ready for the crash we had all expected. The girl's feet were digging into the floorboards and her eyes were shut tight. The cars ahead sorted themselves out and I managed a shaky grin.

'That would have been my fault, of course.'

Neither of them answered. Billboards bathed in sickly yellow gave way to vast suburban complexes, bleak concrete oblongs dotted with lighted windows. We were through Montrouge and at the Port d'Orleans before the girl came to life.

'Would you like to let us off here, please?'

There was an orange shield at the top of some steps. METROPOLITAIN I pulled up in front of it. It was a dreary scene. Neon signs blinking on empty expanses of near-freezing sidewalks.

'You're sure?' I insisted.

She seemed to hesitate then turned up her coat and

opened the door on her side. Her partner was out of the car almost as quickly as she was. Both of them put their heads down and ran for the steps without looking back. Neither of my passengers had offered as much as a smile or a word of thanks. I started the motor again, putting them out of my mind. A reflection in a store-window caught my eye as I waited for the next set of traffic-signals. I turned my head and saw the girl waving frantically. I waved back, glad that she had remembered her manners. Her boyfriend appeared. There seemed to be a brief argument and then they were both gone again. The green light released me. The Renault was halfway across the intersection when I noticed an unfamiliar shape on the back seat. I knew now why she had been waving. They'd left the blue canvas bag behind. There were no cops in sight so I made a U-turn, parked and ran down the Metro steps taking the bag with me. The station was empty except for a crone dressed in some ghastly parody of a ticket-collector's uniform.

'Deux personnes,' I gasped. I was twelve pounds overweight and breathless from the run. *'Un homme et une femme.'*

'Billet,' she barked, jaws opening and shutting like a shark's.

There was nothing for it but to take the bag back to the car and open it. I was hoping to find a name, an address. Inside was a pair of striped flannel pyjamas and some felt-soled slippers, the sort of thing worn by old men in the mountains. It seemed an odd piece of packing for a lovers' weekend. They didn't even have a toothbrush between them. I closed the bag and threw it on the back seat. As a boy scout I was out of practice. The hotel concierge could return the bag to the police.

It was almost six by the time I finally reached the Place des Vosges. To my mind it's the loveliest square in Paris. The lights were on, adding softness to seventeenth-century redbrick facades faced with stone. There are cloistered walks, trees in a central square and a fountain at each corner. Gunn's Hotel is close to the Victor Hugo Museum. There isn't another hotel like it in Paris, probably not in the whole of France. A stranger has no more chance of finding a bed there than he would in Buckingham Palace. There are ten rooms, a bar, no restaurant. The only food served is breakfast. Most of the space is rented on a permanent basis by expensive-looking ladies who mind their own business. As far as that goes, everyone at Gunn's is a model of discretion, including the owner. Most nights of the week, you'll see a few civil-servants in the bar, cops from the vice-squad, some high-echelon gangsters. Despite the dissimilarity there's never any trouble. They're all members of the Union Corse, the secret society that controls the vice and drug rackets throughout the whole of France. Gunn's isn't cheap but they'll launder a shirt for you in twenty minutes and hold an account for a year if necessary. They've nursed me through a fever-ridden bout of pleurisy and rumour has it that the same doctor will heal a gunshot wound without asking questions. George Gunn owns the place.

The way it is with him and me is that we both grew up in the Caledonian Orphanage, Bruce County, Ontario. George is five years older than I am, just the right age for his exploits to have impressed me at a receptive time in my life. In those days, the orphanage used to supply cheap labour to local farmers. Any boy over fifteen put in a twelve-hour day in the fields or barns and did his schoolwork at night. The pay was two-and-a-half dollars a week. The governors of the orphanage copped the rest in payment for the inmates keep. About the time that George went to pick apples for the Elton Fruit Farms, I was struggling with the subtleties of English grammar. Three months later George took off with the farm-manager's daughter, aged seventeen, and the contents of the office safe. The R.C.M.P. picked them up at Hamilton bus-depot, daughter and money intact. I remember clearly how the news came to the Caledonian.

The chapel-bell assembled the entire institution, eighty-five of us. We waited in an atmosphere of damp clothes and mouldy prayerbooks. The overseer was a rawbone Scot from Aberdeen who had all the passion of a Savanarola. He took his place at the lectern, cracking his knuckles till his glare had achieved complete silence. Then he launched himself into a harangue that touched on original sin, the ingratitude of the impoverished young and the inevitablity of God's punishment. Every boy in the chapel followed the account of George's misdeeds with a sense of terror and personal involvement. The Royal Canadian Mounted Police were produced as avenging angels, Springfield Reformatory as the hell for which we were all heading fast. The session closed with an invocation to the Almighty to spare us, miserable sinners, and soften our hearts against the sin of pride. I've never forgotten a word of it.

The years passed. I progressed from working around Frank Stannard's horse-barn to a job as a copyrunner on a Montreal newspaper. Stannard's brother happened to be the publisher and he provided my first real break. In 1960 the London *Post* gave me a three-year contract to come to England and start the Profile Page. Eighteen months later I was in Paris doing a piece on Ilinka Ostrava. It was a hot June and I'd taken my copy to the Piscine Molitor, telling myself that I was working. I must have dozed off, deaf to everything but the splash of water and girls' voices, when someone spoke my name. The sound and locution was vaguely familiar. I opened my eyes to see George Gunn standing in front of me. He was wearing a large-size belly over Bermuda shorts and was grotesquely fat but unmistakably himself.

You don't forget the people you grow up with even if it's in an orphanage. It was suddenly good to sit there in the sunshine, drinking beer off the ice, surrounded by good-looking chicks and remembering the miseries of a generation ago. We dined together that night, exchanging edited accounts of the intervening years. George's tale seemed to me to be especially full of gaps but I figured that to be his affair. The fact that he owned a hotel in Paris was proof enough of respectability and success. I fell into the habit of staying there every time I came to the city. It was comfortable, centrally-located and George gave me a deal on the rates.

I locked the Renault and carried the blue canvas bag into the hotel with me. George's nose had led him to the right architect. The conversion from seventeenth-century mansion to hotel has been done with great taste. The courtyard became the lobby, the coachman's lodge the bar. A narrow elevator-shaft pierces what once was the central staircase and place has been found to instal eight bathrooms. George lives up in the penthouse with his tropical fish and hi-fi equipment. There are no travel posters in the lobby, no airline or oil company calendars. There's a large leather settee opposite the reception desk, a hanging fragrance that's a reminder of the elegant ladies upstairs and a set of Dufy racetrack prints on the walls. In winter the hotel is always warm.

The door to the bar was open, the rose-coloured interior inviting. The man on duty at the desk was a barrel-chested Ukrainian who has been with George from the beginning. I put the bag down. There was no sign of the concierge.

'What happened to Phillippe?' I asked.

Mikhail reached behind for my room key. It was Sunday so his clothes smelled of incense. He sings in the choir at the Greek Orthodox church.

'Only the poor work on the seventh day,' he intoned in his *basso profundo*. 'The underprivileged people of the world.'

'Sure,' I said 'I've just finished four hours of it.' I held my hand out for the slip of paper he was offering.

He nodded in the direction of the bar. 'M. Gunn would like a word with you.'

Except for George and the barman the place was empty. Mario faded away as soon as I came in. George was on his feet. No barstool ever made is any use to him. He's six feet four inches tall and weighs two hundred and eighty pounds. His butt falls over a stool in the same way as cake-dough oozes over the top of a mould. Like everything else that he wears, his dark-brown suit was custom-made. The remnants of his rusty-coloured hair is combed forward in a kind of Friar Tuck arrangement. Small restless eyes greeted me.

'Where the hell have you been all day?' he challenged.

'Texier,' I said. 'You wanted to see me?'

'You're damn right,' he said, scratching his back against the edge of the bar. There's a suggestion of ponderousness about him that leads some people to think that George is a slow thinker. Nothing could be further from the truth. When George thinks it is fast and to the purpose. 'Did you get your message at the desk? Some woman's been calling you all afternoon.' He levelled his eyes on the slip of paper in my hand, expecting me to open it. I did no such thing.

'It happens,' I said, putting him on. 'Every once in a long long while, it happens, George.'

He withdrew his head like a scared tortoise. 'You remember what I told you last night?'

There'd been this chick in the bar, a busty brunette I had thought to be alone. I was well into a routine line with her when I caught George's face in the mirror. He was sitting with a couple of Corsican heavies. All three were watching me. I dropped the whole thing, excused myself and went up to my room. Later on, George exposed the facts to me. The girl was a singer in a nightclub, the guy her boyfriend. His name was the French equivalent of Icepick Willie or something.

I lifted my head. 'If you're thinking about the singer, George. The answer is positively no. I got the message last night.'

His tone was grudging. 'If you're lying you're crazy. That chick is deadly.' He drew his thumb across his gullet suggestively.

I unfolded the piece of paper and let him see it. *Dinner at nine and don't keep me waiting.* Ilinka never bothers to put her name to a message and with me it isn't necessary.

'Don't tell me you haven't already seen it,' I said. 'The lady has the best legs in Paris but she happens to be sixty-nine years of age. Why don't you stop worrying about me.'

He snorted. 'The company you keep, somebody has to,' He grins like a ventriloquist's dummy, the bottom half of his face slicing up somewhere round his nose.

'You must be kidding,' I said. 'You're the most self-centred man in the city.' The truth was that in a strange way we were family. We had shared cold and hunger and neither of us was likely to forget it.

George's grin faded. 'So how did you make out with Texier?'

I shrugged. 'Nothing to it. Jean-Paul's one of those people who knows that what he's done is good and doesn't bother to tell you. There are only a few of us left.'

I walked across the lobby and asked Mikhail to put a call through to London. The phone was ringing by the time I reached the fourth floor. I kneed the door shut and sat down on the bed. It was Joe Hayter on the line, an oldtimer and a friend. The first London edition goes to press at eleven o'clock at night but if Joe had his way he would sleep at his desk.

'Ross Macintyre,' I said. 'You want to leave a message on Misty's desk for me?' A thought struck me. 'She wouldn't be in the building by any chance?'

'That is rich,' he said with heavy sarcasm. 'Weekend and our ace feature man asks if his Girl Friday is in the building! What the hell would she be doing here any more than you would? If that's all you wanted to know, get off the line and stop wasting the firm's money. I'm busy.'

'We all know your dedication,' I told him. 'The message is that I'll be back tomorrow afternoon, sixteen-thirty hours at Heathrow. Tell her to arrange transport.' I hung up quickly before his reply broke my eardrums.

I could have called Misty at home but that would have meant trouble. She resents every minute that I spend with Ilinka and would have wanted to have known what I was doing. Lying only complicates matters. Feet up on the bed, I closed my eyes for a few minutes, thinking about the evening ahead. I find Ilinka the most exciting woman in Paris. She's a *grande dame* in the French tradition, widow of a Czech historian and more fun than a clutch of the chicks from Castel's. She has survived two violent upheavals in her life to become an institution in a country that isn't her own. Doors open mysteriously for her. The fact that she is a Commander of the Legion of Honour surely helps. I had done a profile on her nine years before and fallen in love. She was the mother I didn't remember, the wife I'd never had, the standard by which I judged other women. Added to that, she never stops telling me that one day I'll make a writer.

I kicked off my shoes and sprawled lower. The bedrooms at Gunn's were designed with women in mind. My room had light grey walls and a lavender carpet. The mattresses are an invitation to linger. A colour-television set fitted into a wall-niche at the ends of the two beds. I switched it on and started a bath. The bathrooms are on the small side but they have deep pile carpets and black marble makeup tables furnished with lotions and scents that are on the house. One of George's Corsican chums is a cosmetic wholesaler. I lowered myself into the steaming water, vaguely listening to the newscast from the other room. The announcer's voice suddenly took on the nasal urgency of a Walter Winchell.

L'Affaire Brown made the headlines again when

Radnor Brown escaped from Fresnes Prison hospital early this afternoon. Brown, an American subject, has been held for medical observation since August pending investigation of a charge of attempted rape. Security guards making a routine check of the ward missed Brown shortly after the midday meal had been served. A rope-ladder was found attached to the wall that encloses the prison garden. Accomplices are known to have been waiting for Brown outside with clothing and transport. Later this afternoon, the authorities removed a red Austin minicar that had been abandoned near Chapelle-Noisy. The Police Judiciare is conducting a full-scale inquiry into the escape and wish to interview the driver of a Renault 16 seen in the area at the same time.

The words sliced through my lethargy like a hot fly through butter. I grabbed a towel and pounded into the bedroom just in time to catch the mug-shot coming up on the screen. The police-photograph showed a spectacled face that I recognised only too well. I stood there, the water dripping off my body on to the carpet, till the image was replaced by a filmed picture of the red mini being towed away. I had a horrible feeling that the next photograph might well be of me. The commercial that followed only partly put my mind at rest. I found a pack of cigarettes and my lighter. The implications hit like blows with a bludgeon. I had aided and abetted, as the saying goes, a criminal to escape justice. My first thought was for the Renault. I looked down from the window, expecting to see the car surrounded by cops. The light from the hotel portico shone across a lonely stretch of pavement. I let the curtain fall and sat down on the bed again. The obvious thing to do was to go to the police and put this on a sane footing. I could explain what had happened – anyone with an ounce of consideration would have acted in the same way as I had, I'd say. Reflection poked a hole in this line of thought. I imagined the look on some hardnosed cop's face as he reminded me that a hundred other drivers had passed the stalled mini without stopping. The interview would become an inquisition. French law operates on the assumption that a suspect is guilty. I could quite easily spend the next few days trying to produce myself as a person of impeccable background and a true friend of the Republic.

I dried my feet on the edge of the basin, suddenly aware of a more urgent reason for keeping my mouth shut. The events had all the makings of a story. I buzzed the desk and told Mikhail to get me the *Post* Paris bureau. An answering-service provided a Passy number. Mickey Longman's holler sounded above a background of children's screams. I blocked one ear. I knew Longman from a dozen French assignments.

I identified myself. 'Hi, Mickey. What do you know about Radnor Brown, the guy who was just on the news?'

A door slammed violently. 'These bloody kids,' he said bitterly. 'What was that again?'

I gave him the name once more, amplifying. 'The Fresnes Prison break.'

'Oh that!' He managed to make it sound as if I'd been talking through a mouthful of marbles. 'Not too much I'm afraid, old boy. I know we did something on him when he first arrived to work for U.N.S.C.A.D. I seem to remember the human interest angle. "Young scientist chooses life of public service." You know the sort of thing.'

I did and it wasn't what I wanted. 'Can you remember if he had a wife?' A wife who's an excellent liar, I thought, recalling how the girl had said Brown spoke no English.'

'Look, old boy,' Longman said wearily. 'That piece was written a couple of years ago. How the hell can I be expected to remember whether or not the man has a wife?

'Why don't you come round in the morning if it's that important. There's certainly something in the files.'

'I need the information tonight,' I answered. 'Is there any way of me getting into the office now?'

His voice sounded as if I'd made an indecent proposal. '*Now?* It's Sunday, old boy. What is all this about anyway?'

'Idle curiosity,' I answered. I didn't much care what he thought. 'Do I get in or not?'

'I suppose I could call the building-superintendent,' he said reluctantly. 'See you turn off all the lights.'

I hung up thinking that if the regular crime man ever got wind of the story he'd be over on the next flight wearing his sleuth's hat. I wanted this one for myself. I was here, sitting on it, and I knew I could handle it better than anyone else. I raised Mikhail again and gave him Ilinka's number.

'It's me, darling, Ross. Look, I can't explain now but I'm not going to be able to make it for dinner. I'll call you later. O.K.?'

Her consonants clang like steel gates and her 'r's roll. 'I shall only forgive you if I found out she is pretty and not intelligent. Perhaps not even then. Pig!'

'It's business, Ilinka,' I said firmly. 'I'll call you later.'

I cleaned up my shoes and sweater. I'd brought along an old suede golfing jacket that I put on over the sweater. I checked my pockets for money, passport and presscard. Two things had to be done quickly. The first was to get rid of Brown's prison gear and the bag, the second was to return the rented Renault. The bag came first for obvious reasons. Once it was off my hands, I could safely plead ignorance. Sure I gave some people a lift, but fugitives from justice, you must be kidding, officer! That was the general idea, anyway.

I opened the door stealthily. It was better that I left the hotel without being seen with the bag. It was a quarter-of-seven. The only other room on the floor was occupied by a Greek opera-singer. George described her somewhat cryptically as the friend of a friend. I'd ridden the elevator up with her once, a tall woman with a drowned face rising out of a sable collar. I tiptoed along the corridor to the passdoor. A back staircase leads down to the kitchen area which is directly behind the bar. Copper pans, no longer used except as decoration, gleamed on the walls. Three maids and a Portuguese houseboy come on duty at eight in the morning and work through till six. Tomorrow's breakfast trays were already prepared on the kitchen table.

The back door operates on a spring-lock. I let myself out into a small cobbled yard lined with garbage cans. Another door gives access to Rue de Birague. There were few people about and the Paris roar was noticeable, made up of the noise of the traffic, the boats on the river, the jets stacked overhead.

I turned the corner on to Rue St Antoine in time to see a cab coming at me fast. Cabdrivers operating the night-shift in Paris are supposed to face a one-in-ten chance of a stickup. This guy slowed, giving me a hard look before he finally stopped and wound his window down.

'Ou allez-vous?'

'Aux Invalides, the air-terminal.'

He jerked his head, indicating me to climb in. He reported his destination to the dispatcher. He drove the way they all do, bluffing his way across intersections, taking the bends as if he could see round them. The air-terminal is in the north-east corner of a vast open space over on the Left Bank, just south of the river. I paid off the hack and walked into the arrival-hall. I've never seen the place other than crowded. The benches are always full of unshaven men and women with eyes like poached eggs. Porters are a thing of the past. I took the blue bag over to a pay-locker, put the key in an envelope marked TO BE CALLED FOR and left it at the Information Desk. It was out of the way but available.

It was gone eight by the time I returned the Renault to the rental company's pickup point. A girl with a bad headcold received me. She walked round the car hurriedly, copied the details from my charge-card and gave me a form to sign. The street was chilly after the heated office. I made my way to the nearest Metro station. The *Post* bureau is on Rue Lincoln, in a corner-block facing Champs-Elysees. A surly building-superintendent answered the bell and told me that the elevators weren't working. I climbed up six floors and let myself into the suite of rooms. Exotic-looking plants grew in an atmosphere like that of a hothouse. There were flowers on the desks. Way below, the lights receded to the Rond-Point. There was an impression of gracious living that was a long way away from the clamour of the London office. I took my suede jacket off and found Longman's bottle in the bottom drawer of his desk.

The *Post* library is acknowledged to be the best of its kind in Paris. Some bygone bureau-chief started it back in the thirties when the paper ran a Paris edition. Since then the venture has somehow escaped the eyes of the London auditors. All the French newspapers and magazines are on file as well as those from Germany, Italy and Spain. Anything before 1969 has been microfilmed and is stored in cans. I grabbed an armful of material and sat down. The piece Longman had mentioned was dated 12th January, 1970.

HONOURS STUDENT SETS SIGHTS ON PUBLIC SERVICE

PARIS

Radnor Brown, 28, a Faraday Award winner described as one of the years most brilliant students at M.I.T. flew into town today from Boston. He follows in the tradition of a number of dedicated scientists who have joined the staff of the United Nations Scientific Aid and Development Organization. Mr. Brown will specialize in the culture of germ-resistant grains and intends making a temporary home with his sister on the Quai de Bourbon. Phoebe Brown is a graduate of Luisiana State University and currently studying art under the painter Max Bulgakov.

I found a pencil and paper. The entries I wanted were in the telephone directory.

BROWN, Phoebe. 235 Quai de Bourbon 4e.

BULGAKOV, Maximilien. 76 Square Louvois 2e.

I took a sheaf of French newspapers and concentrated on the month of August, 1971. I found the first reference to Brown on the 18th.

AMERICAN ACCUSED OF SEXUAL ASSAULT

Radnor Brown, a United States citizen described as a scientist and giving an address in Neuilly-sur-Seine was arrested late last night and appeared this morning before Examining-Magistrate M. Etienne Colombes. The complainant, Mlle. Claire de Pornic, testified that she had returned late from a concert and had parked her car in the forecourt of her apartment-building. When she walked towards the entrance the accused man leaped on her from the shadows and attempted to drag her into a doorway. Mlle. de Pornic screamed for help, doing her best to fight off the continued attacks of her ravisher. The occupants of a passing car, M. Pierre Pelazzi and Commandant Gilles Kerembrun heard the cries and came to her assistance. The witnesses gave evidence that they found the accused man struggling on the ground with Mlle. de Pornic whose clothing was torn and disarranged. The two men overpowered Brown and summoned the police. Doctor of Medicine, Edouard Charpentier, testified that Mlle. de Pornic's thighs were badly bruised and that the accused had suffered superficial bruises to the head and right shoulder. The Examining-Magistrate ordered Brown to be committed to Fresnes Prison hospital for medical observation.

'Rape' is always a heady word. The classic ploy of the woman with second thoughts is to shout it loud and clear. But the main text of the tale suggested that Brown and the girl were strangers to one another which made him some kind of a spook with a very sick mind.

I found myself thinking about his face, the pale grey eyes behind the spectacles, the narrow mouth. It all fitted well enough if you were prepared to hang a dog by the droop of its tail. I closed the office and returned the keys to the building superintendent. At that stage of the game, I was playing it very cool. Brown's bag was safely out of the way, there was no backlash from the rented car and I was sure that the story was a beat.

The Metro took me as far as Pont-Marie. I surfaced opposite Ile-St-Louis. Men have been heading for islands since the beginning of time, impelled by some atavistic urge. An island in the middle of a capital city offers something very special. Ile-St-Louis is a little under half-a-mile long, three hundred yards across at its widest point. Five bridges join it to the mainland. Most of the people who are born there continue to work in the neighbourhood. The butchers, the bakers, the people who run the cafes and grocery-stores. It's a tight community with a chauvinistic attitude towards the rest of the city. There are a few small hotels run by Vietnamese, a couple of 'So-so' restaurants and a sprinkling of antique stores. The eighteenth-century palaces and mansions facing the quays have long since been converted into elegant apartments. The leases change hands for astronomical sums. Phoebe Brown was lucky to live there even if it was in no more than a lumber-room.

I walked over the bridge and turned right on Quai de Bourbon. From the outside at least, the towering houses look pretty much as they must have done when they were built nearly three hundred years ago. A line of cars was parked up on the sidewalk. Opposite was a stone retaining wall and beyond it steps leading down to the quay. I took a good look at 235 as I passed. A pair of enormous doors reached up, enclosing an interior courtyard. There was a small postern and a bell marked CONCIERGE, a heavily-curtained window at street-level. I stopped at the corner and lit a cigarette. Everything seemed normal enough. People were queueing for tables at the nearby brasserie. A girl leaned from the window and shouted to someone below.

I strolled back and rang the doorbell. Someone inside touched a button and the postern clicked open. The cobbled courtyard was lit by a single lantern high in the vaulted ceiling. An archway led to a smaller yard with some tubs of dingy hydrangeas. A red-carpeted staircase curved up behind a plate-glass window on my right. A woman was standing in a nearby doorway, watching me. She was short and fat and wore a long cardigan that reached way below her hips.

'Vous desirez, Monsieur?' she asked.

I smiled. 'Bon soir, Madame. Mlle Brown?'

She shook her head quickly and decisively. 'Not here, Monsieur.'

It wasn't clear whether she meant that Phoebe Brown was absent or didn't live there at all. I fumbled in my pocket for some money.

'But it is the right address?'

She shook her head again, ignoring the bill in my outstretched hand. 'Mlle Brown is not here, Monsieur.'

The movements on each side of me were sudden and concerted. Two men stepped into the courtyard, one from the shadows on my left, the other from behind the *concierge*. I stand over six feet in my socks but the newcomers topped me by inches. Both were built on the order of good fast heavyweights and were dressed in those dark box-like overcoats. They wore narrow-brimmed hats pulled down over their eyes. The guy on my left drifted round to the postern and put his back against it. His partner sidestepped the concierge, thumbing her back to her quarters. He stopped underneath the lantern, directly in front of me. His ears were flat against his skull and I had the feeling that if he took off his hat his hair would be crewcut. He looked me up and down, dwelling on the corduroy pants and beat-up golfing jacket.

'Police. Vos papiers!'

I gave him my passport and presscard. The concierge's door clicked shut. The cop held the documents to the light, feeling the quality of the paper. The backs of his fingers were covered with coarse black hair.

'Your address in Paris?'

The building had gone strangely quiet. The world outside was completely removed from the scene taking place in the courtyard.

'Place des Vosges,' I replied. 'Gunn's Hotel.'

He tapped on my papers with his nail. It was clean and well-manicured.

'Your business with Mlle Brown, Monsieur?'

I hadn't exactly expected her to be waiting on the doorstep for me. From the moment I'd made up my mind to track her down, an interview with the police had become likely if not inevitable. But there was something about this pair that was positively sinister. I kept my voice courteous.

'You have my presscard in your hand, Monsieur. That should explain my business.'

He glanced across at his partner and read the address on the card aloud making no concession to English pronunciation. I was still pretty certain that I was in the clear. If these men had any idea that I had chauffeured Brown and his sister, their approach would have been very different. The cop smiled as if remembering his manners.

'And of what interest is Mlle Brown to an English newspaper?'

I shrugged. 'That's a question that I can't very well answer till I've spoken to her.'

His eyes were like pebbles at the bottom of a mountain trout-pool, fixed and icy. He chose his words very carefully.

'You came to Paris to interview Mlle Brown?'

I shook my head. 'That's not what I said. As a matter of fact, I'm here for an entirely different reason. It so happened that I was watching television this evening. Like I said, I'm a reporter.' I had just about gone through my entire range of facial expressions. This one was meant to be placatory.

The cop grunted, returned my identification and tapped me on the chest.

'There *is* no story, Monsieur. Neither for you nor anyone else. Remember that.' He jerked his head and his companion pulled the latch on the postern. I stepped out to the street feeling about three feet tall. The impulse to look back and then run for my life was strong. I turned the corner with a profound sense of relief. My feelings about the law haven't changed much in thirty years. The first cop I ever knew was Mr Sawchuk, the Town Constable who coached the orphanage hockey-teams. Sawchuk was an ex-paratrooper with a string of hair-raising war-stories. He had us winning the Bruce County Pewee League Championships in his third season. That night he took us all back to his home underneath the jail and presented the whole team with underwear from a Toronto mail-order house. The red wool longjohns were the first non-institutional articles of clothing I had ever owned. They felt like pure cashmere. Mrs Sawchuk cooked turkey for twelve hungry urchins. There was ice-cream topped with maple-syrup and root-beer to drink. I remember the way Sawchuk's medals gleamed in a case on the wall, the smell of the empty cells when we went upstairs and peeped through the bars. It was years before I saw a cell from the inside and then only once and briefly. An argument in a Montreal night-club cost me two front teeth, a hundred dollars fine and a night in the pokey. Few people in my line of business retain many illusions but I've never had any hang-ups about the police. The interview in the courtyard had left me shaken. I wasn't at all sure that I liked the new experience.

I was walking much quicker by the time I passed the brasserie. The bawling of the singing waiters drifted out on the cold air. I crossed the footbridge to Ile-de-la-Cite. The floodlit mass of Notre Dame towered over the narrow channel of water. I pushed through a heavy felt curtain and stood in a side-aisle. Incense hung in the air, adding to the depth of the shadow. People were kneeling with their eyes on the distant altar. Finally the shakes left my legs and I went outside again. Le Coq Hardi is a discovery of Ilinka's. It's run by a Czech couple who serve the best peppered steak in town. The wife of the owner waits table, he cooks. Candles were guttering on the red-checked tablecloths. Mme Stepka gave me a window-seat and pulled the portable heater nearer. She brought hot rolls, a jar of her own pate and a carafe of red wine. I lit a cigarette and took stock.

It still rankled that the two cops had thrown a scare into me. The more I thought about Radnor Brown the less likely the charge against him seemed. It was a matter of probabilities more than anything. A dedicated scientist with his background just wouldn't attack a strange and unwilling woman unless his mind was unbalanced. The other side of the coin was that innocent men don't usually break jail. His sister's motives were easy to understand.

I finished the Brie and spooned sugar into my coffee. My next visit was with Bulgakov and there was no telling what it would produce. I said goodnight to the Stepkas and walked until I found a cab that took me as far as the Bilbliotheque Nationale. There were few streetlights and the gates to the gardens were locked. I walked round to the south side of the square and looked across the railings at the house where Bulgakov lived. The big studio windows at the top were uncurtained. A shadow lengthened there as I watched. The trees were motionless as if waiting for the snow that had been forecast and the temperature was dropping by the minute. The suede jacket and the wine I had drunk kept me warm. I skirted the railings, my eyes still on the studio windows. The police would surely have been to see Bulgakov. It didn't look as if the place was staked-out but this was a chance that I had to take. There was a pay-phone just round the corner. I dialled Bulgakov's number, keeping one foot in the door in case I had to move fast. A deep, heavily-accented voice answered. Piano music was playing in the background. I recognised it as Scarlatti. Misty has the same record.

'M. Bulgakov?' I asked.

'Lui-meme.' There were no clicks, no sudden echoes, nothing to indicate a tapped line.

'I wanted to see you about some lessons,' I said. 'A friend gave me your name.'

'No lessons,' the voice said quickly. 'No more pupils. I regret, Monsieur, but I can take no more.'

I let my voice slide into a lower register. 'In precisely one minute from now your doorbell will ring. Answer it.'

I hung up and walked round the corner. The catch was released as soon as I pressed the button. I stepped into a dark unheated hallway and groped along the wall until I found the staircase. A shaft of light from the top floor illuminated the banisters. The man waiting for me was dressed in a dirty denim worksuit. He could have been any age between sixty and seventy with grey hair, a crumpled face and Fu-Manchu moustache. He sidled round me like a crab skirting a rock and kicked the door shut. The marks on the wood showed that the exercise was customary. The apartment was on two levels, a small room downstairs with an even smaller kitchen through an arch. A refectory-table was littered with the remains of several meals, a guitar and a scrubbing-brush. Paint-rags smouldered in the fireplace. A ladder gave access to the room upstairs. My host watched me closely with a kind of lunatic stare. His hands were the ugliest I had ever seen, the fingers arthritic, the nails loaded with paint. His smile displayed a bank of stainless steel teeth.

'We do not know one another, Monsieur. What is it that you want from me?'

'Phoebe Brown,' I said.

His cheeks hung in folds, tufts of forgotten bristles half-hidden in the wrinkles. He reached behind at random, taking a piece of cheese from the table. He put it into his mouth without even looking at it and filled a dubious glass from a bottle. I put the glass down. The rough red wine was undrinkable.

'Phoebe Brown,' he mumbled. 'The little American girl. But why come to see me about her?'

'A hunch,' I said, moving away from the stale smell of his clothing.

He came after me, framing my face between his thumb and forefinger and closing one eye.

'An interesting head,' he remarked. 'Very interesting.'

I blocked his forward progress with a hand. 'You can skip the crazy Bohemian act. Your pupil's running herself into deep trouble.'

He drew himself up with melancholy dignity. 'I have already told the officers. I have not seen the girl for five days. Come!'

He led me up the ladder, pointing out the absence of a handrail. The studio had once been an attic. Lights were cut in the sloping roof and the walls had been plastered. There was an enormous unmade bed with dirty sheets, books piled on the floor, dust-covered bric-a-brac, a wax doll and some fans. At the far end of the room, a canvas stood on an easel. A pair of french windows offered access to a shaky home-made balcony outside. The first snowflakes were drifting across the panes down to the square below. Bulgakov wrenched the bed-covers back.

'See,' he said with the same sad dignity. 'She is not here. Nor here!' He opened a small door on a minute bathroom.

I propped myself against the wall, wondering how to get through to him.

'Don't you think you could be making a mistake about me? I want to help the girl.'

'You are wasting your time, Monsieur,' he said.

I came off the wall. 'Why did you open the door to me? Were you expecting someone else – Phoebe's brother, maybe?'

He pointed down the ladder. 'I must ask you to leave, Monsieur. I must work.'

There was a scribbling block by the phone downstairs. I wrote the number of the hotel and shoved it into his reluctant grasp. 'Get this straight in your head, friend. The wolves are after Phoebe and I'm the only one who can save her. See she gets this message. Don't use your phone. Go across the square to the hotel.'

He stood there, fingering his moustache like The Anarchist in an amateur production of Tolstoy.

'Without me, she's dead,' I emphasised and shut the door.

I waited on the corner, hidden by the railings. Two minutes passed and Bulgakov emerged. He hurried round the square and vanished into the hotel. The fall of snow was too light as yet to do more than make the sidewalks damp and uncomfortable. I turned up my collar and walked till I found a cruising cab that took me to Gunn's. I pushed through the revolving doors, shaking the wet from my head and clothes. The bar was a haze of cigar-smoke. I could see George's rusty head presiding at a gathering of his Corsican friends. A couple of overdressed women sat at the table, diamonds flashing as they gesticulated. Nothing on the premises escapes George's eye. His chair was in its usual position, facing the lobby. I knew he had seen me come in. He raised a hand, taking over the conversation. His French is worse than mine. He learnt both accent and idiom in a Quebec lockup and he never gets out of the present tense. It seems to work.

I went across to the reception-desk. Mikhail held his place in his Ukrainian-language newspaper and attended to my inquiry.

'No, Monsieur. No messages.'

'I'm expecting a call,' I said casually. 'I'll be upstairs in my room. Put it through.'

It was half-an-hour before the phone rang. I recognised the voice immediately.

'You know who I am?' I asked.

'I know, yes.' The response was very quiet.

'Are you alone – you're sure nobody's following you?'

'Pretty sure.' She sounded as if she'd asked herself the same question too many times.

It was snug there in the bedroom, insulated from the slicing snow. I brought the mouthpiece closer.

'Listen carefully. The police are crawling all over your apartment. Your concierge has probably described the clothes you were wearing. Have you thought about that?'

'Yes, I have.'

I heard the noise of a train in the background. 'Where are you speaking from?' I demanded quickly.

She hesitated and then told me. 'Gare Montparnasse.'

I thought for a second, getting the neighbourhood in focus. 'O.K. There's an all-night cafeteria right across from where you are, a big neon sign that says PARIS-MANGE. Are you with me?'

I heard her open the door of the booth, the noise from

outside. 'Yes. I can see it from here.'

'Hang up and get yourself over there,' I said. 'And keep away from the windows. I'll be with you as soon as I can.'

The only other protection I had against the weather was a nylon anorak. I zipped it up and went down to the lobby. The cigar-smoke was thicker but George caught my exit. I knew he'd be wondering about my dinner date. Falling snow made the lights of Montparnasse blurred and watery. Caped cops were busy at the intersections, reinforcing the traffic-signals with blasts on their whistles. The bars and restaurants were still doing business. I picked my way through gathering slush. The plate-glass windows of the automat were steamed and the place stank of sauerkraut.

Any mainline station in any big city has its PARIS-MANGE and the customers are stock. Seventy-five per cent of them are provincials waiting for an early morning train, morose hookers pondering the prospect of a scoreless night, the unimportant and dispossessed stretching their cups of coffee as far as they dare. I took my place on the line and located Phoebe Brown sitting alone at a table. She had tied her bright hair in a scarf and was reading a newspaper. I came round behind her and pulled the vacant chair. She looked up, her hand going to her throat, her green eyes startled. Her fingers were well-shaped, the nails trimmed short and without varnish. She was wearing a belted raincoat.

I put my cup of coffee on the table and leaned forward. 'Have you changed your clothes since you left your apartment?'

She nodded. 'Max said you wanted to see me.'

I smiled for the benefit of the woman at the next

table. 'That was quite a production this afternoon. Congratulations!'

She half closed her eyes, her face drawn in the harsh lighting. 'What did you expect us to do, tell you the truth?'

'People are watching us,' I warned. 'Try to look as if you're enjoying this conversation.'

She managed a shaky smile. 'You can't really be serious.'

'I'm serious,' I said. 'Don't you realise that what you're doing is crazy. When the law catches up with you, they'll try you as an accessory.'

'I know it,' she said in a small voice. 'I've always known it.'

'That makes it even worse,' I argued. 'Look, trust me and it needn't happen. I want to help you.'

She gave the statement some thought before turning her mouth down on it.

'Why would you want to help me?'

'Not just you,' I answered. 'Your brother, too. I work for a newspaper and the name is Ross. Let me hear you say it one time!'

'Ross,' she said tremulously. Her nerve was running out fast. It showed in her eyes, the way her hands were trembling.

I tightened my grip. 'Look, I've read the files on this thing and if there's one thing I do know it's my probabilities. There's no way that this case against your brother could hang together. It just wouldn't make sense unless he's very sick. *Is* he sick?'

She pushed her cup aside. 'No. He's not sick.'

'Then give me the real story,' I urged. 'It's the price you pay for the help.'

The woman with a string-bag full of melons at the next table was almost falling off her chair in an effort to hear. Phoebe gave me the same shaky grin.

'The real story. Where would you want me to begin?'

'Wherever it starts,' I said. 'Look, I'm ready to take your brother to the best criminal lawyer in the city and if he's innocent we'll get him off. But he'll have to turn himself in first.'

She shook her head decisively. 'He'd never do it. Not now.'

I let her hands go. 'Why not, if he's innocent? Or maybe he isn't – maybe the woman's telling the truth.'

Her face flamed the colour of poinsettia leaves. 'Nothing they've printed about Rad is true. If you knew him, you'd realise how grotesque it all is.'

I gave her a cigarette and lighted it for her. 'You need someone to rap with. Why not tell me about it?'

She picked a shred of tobacco from her tongue. 'I wish I'd never listened, about the jailbreak, I mean. Not for my sake, for Rad's. What in the world is going to happen to him now?'

It was a good question. I took a sip of lukewarm coffee and tried again, easily, as if it were a matter of small importance.

'Where's Rad now?'

She looked at her fingers for a while. 'Do you know what it is to be alone in a city without one single person being on your side?'

'I know,' I answered.

She must have believed me. 'It had to be today or never. Rad's escape, that is. It was something to do with the guard who was on duty. Rad relied on me. I just couldn't let him down. I went to Max in desperation.

Rad's in the atelier. We've got to get out in the morning. Max has his classes.'

I shook my head in wonder. She had as much right in this sort of caper as I had climbing into the ring with Joe Frazier.

'It sounds like a real screwball operation that ought to land you both in jail within a matter of hours. Don't you ever think?'

She was very close to tears. 'When you're on the run, there's no time to think. I learned that today.'

Something about the place, the people round us, emphasised the hopelessness of the whole venture. I thought seriously about getting up, walking away and not looking back.

She must have sensed something because she raised her hand and let it fall.

'It doesn't matter. I don't even care any more.'

I took her wrist again. 'That's crap. Look, I'm no knight in shining armour. I'm not even a crime-reporter. I'm just a guy playing a hunch. If it pays off, I'll probably ask the management for more money.'

Her eyes were uncertain. 'Do you *really* mean what you said about helping us?'

'Of course I mean it. What do you think I'm doing here?' I argued. 'I could have turned the lot of you in, Bulgakov included. I've told you what I'm prepared to do. The rest is up to you.'

'I'm sorry,' she said quietly. 'Sorry I doubted you. You're very kind, sir.'

'Yes or no?' I demanded. She seemed to me to be lost in the Deep South at the moment.

Her eyes searched mine then she folded her newspaper. 'I'll take you to him.'

Outside, the snow was still coming down, fat flakes that clung to the skin before dissolving. The possibility that she had been followed was still on my mind as we went down the steps to the Metro. I took her hand and ran her through a maze of corridors, changing direction and train at the very last moment. We surfaced at Boulevard St Michel, no more than half-a-mile away from her apartment. She hooked her arm through mine and we dashed through the slush-spattering traffic. She led me into a cul-de-sac behind the Cluny Museum. A solitary streetlamp lit a row of lockup garages, a second-storey building overhead that was reached by an outside iron staircase. The blank wall opposite formed the back of the museum. We climbed the stairs and she opened the door with a key. It was even colder inside than out and in complete darkness. I heard her lock the door again and fumble for the light switch.

'Rad?' she called softly.

A light came on in the corner. The long bare room ran the entire length of the cul-de-sac. Lengths of burlap masked the windows. Scattered around were the props of an art-school, still-life models, plaster figures, lengths of drapery. A battered kerosene heater spluttered near the light. Standing beside it was Radnor Brown, still wearing his checked mackinaw and pointing a small shiny gun at my stomach. Something, snow probably slithered down the roof and fell below.

Phoebe stepped between us quickly. 'He's trying to help us, Rad!'

Brown had acquired another dimension suddenly. I remembered the saying: a desperate man is more dangerous than a hero. He stepped round his sister, watching me carefully.

'You must be out of your mind, bringing this man here.'

She pulled off her scarf and shook her hair free. They were both as up tight as could be. It showed in their voices, the way they looked at each other.

'You told me to go, to see what he wanted. The police are everywhere. They've been to the apartment, to see Max. He's scared, Rad. They can take his residence-permit away.'

'I'm sorry,' he said in a stony voice. 'You should have thought of that before.'

I thought for a minute that he'd set her alight but she kept things under control.

'At least listen to what this man has to say,' she pleaded.

'The man's name's Ross Macintyre,' I said. 'I work for the London *Post*.'

His tongue touched the edge of his mouth. 'And suppose I don't like what you have to say?'

I spread my hands. 'I'll leave. Don't worry about me. Your bag's at the air-terminal.' There was a loaf and some cheese on the table.

Brown tapped out a cigarette and stuck it between his lips. The gun he was holding looked about as lethal to him as it did to me.

'Did you give him that thing?' I asked the girl.

She covered the nickelplated automatic with both hands. 'Put it away,' she entreated.

He dropped the gun in a pocket of his mackinaw. His voice came jerkily.

'You're not catching us at our best. What is it you want from us?'

His sister's hands were never far from him, soothing

and restraining, her own tension forgotten in the need to care for his.

'He's already told you, honey,' she wheedled. 'He's a reporter. His newspaper will help you.'

'Since when,' he said heavily, 'does a newspaper *help* people?'

I weighed in, using the same arguments I had on her. He listened, restless under her touch. He shook his head when I had done.

'The way you put it, it sounds a fair proposition. You want my story in return for your help. You don't know what you're taking on, Macintyre. Look – I worked at U.N.S.C.A.D. for almost two years. In that time you get to know people. I was *godfather* to somebody's kid.'

He took off his glasses and blew his nose. 'Not one of my colleagues could bring himself to come to the jail and see me. That includes the father of my goddaughter. What do you think about *that*? Sure, nobody came right out and said to Phoebe "Look your brother's a freak, a rapist!" They just talked about overwork and overstrain. Even the people from the consulate visited me with clips on their noses. For these people I'm *dead*, Macintyre. It's not just people I thought were my friends. It's the police, the Examining Magistrate, everybody. Go ahead and tell me how you're going to break that down!'

The kerosene stove was smelling. I turned it off. Brown's eyes pleaded for the impossible.

'We can always try,' I answered steadily. 'And the way you tell it, there's nothing to lose. We'll assume that you're innocent...'

He cut in sharply, his face flaming. 'It's no assumption. I *am* innocent.'

'You *are* innocent,' I amended. 'Then why are all these people lying?'

His shoulders rose and fell despondently. 'I have a theory. But I couldn't even begin to prove it.'

I checked my watch. It was getting late but he had to talk and I had to listen.

'Let me hear the theory. We'll get around to the proof later.' It was confident stuff but that was the way I was feeling.

Brown must have lain awake at night, re-creating the past and honing his tale to the essentials. It came out soberly, each word driven home with the ring of truth.

'July this year. I was working out at U.N.S.C.A.D. A Colombian chemist had the lab next to mine. He and I had little enough in common. His project was flower-essences. I was doing a survey of germ-resistant grains. We'd meet in the corridor or in the canteen, down on the parking-lot, this kind of thing but we never had a conversation that amounted to anything. Then one day he didn't show for work. The Garde-Champetre found him in his car, deep in Fontainebleau Forest. The motor was still running and Bernanos was dead. There was a length of hose by his side. The other end was attached to the exhaust. A few hours later, the police arrived at the U.N.S.C.A.D. building and started asking about his friends, did anyone know of a motive for his suicide – that kind of stuff. The police interviewed us in Carnot's office, he's the Director of Security. Bernanos came out as a loner with no friends, no women. I heard later that the Colombian Embassy paid for his funeral and we all subscribed to a wreath. The whole affair seemed forgotten. A couple of weeks went by and I was in the storeroom. There's one at the end of each corridor. The usual thing is to indent for what you need and the storeman brings it round. For some reason or other the man wasn't there and I needed pipets in a hurry.'

He paused as if gauging the effect of his tale. I made a sound of understanding. I've been in enough of these conversations to know the danger of criticism, the chance word that will turn the speaker off. True or false, a story gets to be a very personal thing. Brown took it up again.

'I knew where things were kept. I opened up the glass-store. The pipets and bunsen-burners were crated in wood-shavings. I wanted a certain length of rod and I had to dig in deep – to shift some of the crates. Suddenly I could feel a thickness of paper. I went in further. Wedged between two crates was an envelope.'

He lit a cigarette from the stub between his fingers. It was so cold in the studio that our breath was forming vapour. He nodded almost defiantly.

'There was writing, an inscription on it. "To be opened in the event of my death. Juan Bernanos." Well, he was dead all right and I was curious. I opened the envelope. Inside were a couple of sheets of typescript, three Polaroid colour-prints and a newspaper clipping. The pictures were all of the same guy walking on the street, standing outside what looked like a public building of some kind – a courthouse maybe and under the trees at Longchamps. Whoever took those pictures had managed to get in everything, the Runners and Riders board, the name of the track, even the date.'

He told his story well, his eyes never leaving my face. 'The typescript was a detailed description of the heroin that Bernanos had processed and delivered over the previous eighteen months. The amounts and the dates.'

He seemed to have finished. 'You've forgotten the newspaper clipping,' I prompted.

He aimed a stream of smoke between his knees. 'It was from an English daily, it could have been *The Times*, I'm not sure. Anyway it was a report quoting the C.I.A. as saying that the French Secret Service was tied up with a gang smuggling heroin into the States.'

It was a reporter's dream. The unsigned tip-off that flutters through the mailbox, the anonymous whisper over the phone.

'I remember,' I said and I did. 'There was this ex-diplomat who went on the air over Radio Luxembourg and named names, just around the same time.'

'Right,' said Brown. 'Now I want you to get this absolutely clear in your mind. I joined U.N.S.C.A.D. because I believe in what it stood for, the development of science for the benefit of mankind. O.K. I was a square if you like but I had no political hangups, red, blue or pink. What I'd seen in that envelope made me want to puke.'

I was getting the picture all right but I needed more. 'By this time you'd already made up your mind that Bernanos was guilty?'

He wiped his hand across his forehead. In spite of the cold he was sweating.

'I'd made up my mind. I was back in the lab by then, the doors locked. Morphine base is odourless and tasteless. It requires great care and total lack of haste to turn it into heroin. Forget the details but in order to produce a powder that's soluble in water you run the risk of toxic fumes and explosion. The chemist has to be highly proficient. Bernanos *was* highly proficient. What's more, he worked alone and without supervision.'

The girl touched his sleeve. 'The acetic whatever . . .'

Brown seemed to have shrunk inside the bulky mackinaw. 'Acetic anhydride. It only has two purposes. The distillation of perfume and the processing of heroin. The chemists who manufacture it in France are required by law to supply the police with a list of their customers. Bernanos had a perfect cover.'

'Go on,' I urged. I wanted to know how all this tied in with the rape charge. He made his own pace, hunched forward with his hands on his knees.

'Over a thousand people work at U.N.S.C.A.D. Some of them are doing work that is classified on atomic-power projects and the like. Everyone on the establishment is screened before he's accepted. You take an oath that you won't give interviews to the press or discuss your work with the general public. My duty, at least as I saw it, was to report what I'd found to the Chief of Security. But Carnot was in Bonn on some conference or other. So I took the envelope home with me that night and called him from the apartment. He sounded as shocked as I was. It was easy to understand his anxiety. You see, most of U.N.S.C.A.D.'s funds come from the United Nations. Some of the big trusts pick up a few of the tabs. The sort of scandal I had uncovered could have had far-reaching political implications. Carnot's instructions were for me to say nothing about the envelope to anyone – to keep it somewhere safe until he returned from Germany. He was due back in thirty-six hours.'

'And you lost the envelope,' I said quietly.

His face dropped with surprise. 'How could you possibly know that? There wasn't a word of any of this in the newspapers. I hadn't said anything. I didn't dare.'

'It makes a better story,' I said. 'So back comes Carnot and there's no envelope for him. What then?'

He frowned. 'Phoebe and I come from a small town in Louisiana. My great-grandfather built the sawmills. My father was the town doctor. You could say that we both had sheltered lives as children. What the hell would I know about drug-rings. I'd never been in a fist-fight. The truth was that I was scared. I took that envelope, stuck a label over Bernanos' scribble and mailed the thing to myself in care of Paramount Express, Avenue de l'Opera. That's the travel agency. The day Carnot was supposed to be back from Bonn I went to collect the letter. It just wasn't there.'

I put my finger to my lips and tiptoed to the window. A man standing with his back to me below zipped-up, shivered and walked away, his hat and shoulders sprinkled with snow. Brown's hand was still in his sister's.

'So you went back the next day,' I suggested. 'Thinking the mail had been delayed?'

Brown shook his head as if remembering something that was best left forgotten.

'I didn't have to go back. The mail-clerk told me what had happened. It was a temporary job for him. He was one of these kids working his way round the world. The letter had arrived all right. He described the label I used, the colour of the paper. But he'd sent the envelope on to Hong Kong. It seemed that there'd been this other Brown around for the past five or six weeks, in and out the office every day, bugging the kid about his mail. The very day I'd put my letter in the mail, the other Brown dropped by the travel agency with the news that he was leaving Paris. The forwarding address was the Paramount Express, Hong Kong. And that's where my letter went.'

'But the guy's initials weren't the same as yours, surely?' I objected.

Brown made a sign of defeat. 'We never got into that. The letter was gone and that's all there was to it. I understood how it happened. The clerk was just thankful to get this guy off his back. I could have made the same mistake myself.'

Something wasn't jelling. 'How about Carnot?' I asked. 'Couldn't he have used his influence with the postal authorities? They could have pulled that letter out of circulation.'

Phoebe answered for her brother. 'As far as we know Carnot tried. It was too late. Airmail for the Far East had already left France. I was in the travel agency the morning after Rad's arrest. Two men had been there before me, supposedly from the police. No-one seems to know what they said to the mail-clerk but the moment they left he closed his desk and vanished. Nobody's ever seen him again. He didn't even come back to collect his money. The people at Paramount refuse to discuss it, even the manager.'

They looked like a pair of strayed sheep, hearing the baying of the wolves without the wit to plan a defence. I thought quickly.

'Is there a phone in the place, what's the address?'

The girl told me, nodding at a curtain drawn across an embrasure. 'The phone's there.'

Someone had left a piece of gum stuck to the mouthpiece. A torn bra dangled from the hook. Some art-classes. I dialled Ilinka's number.

'I need your help,' I said the moment I heard her

voice. There's nothing particularly sweet about her laugh. It can be bawdy or scornful as it was now but always it's vital.

'You do?' She purred. 'Has the young lady sent you packing?'

Her English is like a 1930 Rolls, perfect in structure and design but a generation out-of-date.

'You're giving a girl a bed for a couple of nights,' I said. 'And not a word to anyone, understand. Will you do it for me or not?'

She never hides her feelings. 'Are you in trouble?' she asked immediately.

'The girl is,' I answered. 'The police. I'll give you the details later. Get one of your friends to pick me up.' I gave her the address.

The White Russian scene in Paris is strictly for the tourists. There are few emigres left. A simple sum supplies the reason. The revolution was fifty-five years ago and all the samovars and violins won't alter the fact. Baritones born in Menilmontant may well sing of a Mother Russia they never even saw, there are not many genuine survivors. Ilinka knows most of them. One runs a car-hire service.

It was typical that she asked no questions. Enough for her that she could smell danger and intrigue. I didn't have to see her face to know that she was enjoying herself. I pulled the curtain back. It was no good asking either of the Browns to make decisions, they had to be driven.

'I'm taking Phoebe to a woman I know, a woman who can be trusted. You'll come with me.'

He was cold, scared and hunted but he still had thought for her. She touched his hand, producing a smile from some unexpected reserve.

'Did anyone ever tell you that you're a good man?'

I nodded. 'Frequently. It comes from a religious upbringing. Transport's on its way. Let's get to the end of the story. You'd just told Carnot that the envelope was missing.'

His breath was fogging his spectacles. He took them off, polished the lens and held them to the light like a spinster checking her crystal. He settled the spectacles back on his nose.

'Carnot listened. He said no more than you have except at the very end. "I'll see you in the morning," he said. I left the room with the damndest feeling that he hadn't believed a word that I'd told him. It wasn't a pleasant feeling. I was having dinner with Phoebe that night. Up to then I hadn't said a word to her about the envelope but the interview with Carnot had me worried. I told her everything. We must have broken up around midnight. I drive a Volkswagen convertible. It was August and the top was down. My apartment was on Rue Galerie de Restraint. I took the Pont du Garigliano and made a left on Michel-Ange. By that time it was getting on for one and there wasn't much traffic about. There's this bad corner opposite the cemetery. I slowed almost to a halt. That's when this black sedan drew up alongside with two men in it. Before I knew what was happening, one of them was in the Volks, sticking a gun into my ribs. The other followed in the sedan. We passed a few other cars. I even saw a couple of cops. I can remember thinking that if I yelled it would be the last time I drew breath. We must have gone a mile. It was still Auteuil but we were much nearer the Bois de Boulogne. Suddenly the guy ordered me to pull on to a parking-lot in front of an apartment-building. He beeped the horn and this girl came out of the front entrance. I'd never seen her before in my life. The rest you know. These guys roughed me up and the police arrived.'

They both looked at me apprehensively as if expecting to find doubt. I believed every word of the story but unsupported by proof he wouldn't have gotten it past a jury of girl-guides.

'What about your apartment?' I asked. 'Anything happen there?'

'It was wrecked,' the girl said. 'Beds overturned, carpets pulled up, even the flour and sugar cans had been emptied. While I was tidying up, they did the same thing to my place. There was nothing taken. Just the same it was horrible.'

'What about Carnot?' I said.

It was a relief to see that Brown could smile. 'Carnot denied every single word. He told Phoebe that the call I made to Bonn had been a complaint about being watched. I'm supposed to have told him that people were following me. A complaint that was completely groundless, he said. He claimed that I'd been acting oddly for some time but that he hadn't realised just how serious things were.'

'What about the envelope?'

His smile withered. 'He told Phoebe that he'd never heard of any envelope.'

She moved her head, agreeing. 'He was kind and gentle. As if he really wanted to help Rad. That's what made the whole visit spooky and sinister. He kept talking about the damage that sexual repression can do, the need to get Rad under treatment. He was going to use his influence with the court to have Rad taken to this clinic in Zurich where they handle these cases. I only saw him the once. He explained that he couldn't go to see Rad in prison for policy reasons.'

'How about the consul – didn't you tell him any of this?'

'What was the good?' Brown's voice was bitter. 'He made up his mind about me the moment he read the newspapers. He's *sure* that I'm guilty. He told me the best thing to do was face facts no matter how ugly they were. With any sort of luck I'll just be deported, he says. You think that's enough for your scoop?'

'They don't say that any more,' I told him. 'The word's a "beat". It's enough. How many other people have you talked to about this? I mean the way you've talked to me?'

'Nobody,' he said flatly. 'There's no-one except you and Phoebe. I've been too scared. They kept coming into the cell – even at Fresnes in the hospital – warning me about perjury. The suggestion was that if I pleaded guilty the sentence would be deportation.'

I had my story all right. I was sure of it now. 'Look,' I said. 'This is going to be a two-way operation. First of all we have to trust one another. The next thing is that I call the shots. Agreed?'

He pushed out his hand, his smile part gratitude, part nervousness. 'Like you said, I've nothing to lose.'

I threw the bread and cheese out and Brown replaced the light bulbs. As far as I could see there was no sign left that we had been there. No matter how good a friend Bulgakov was, the police were going to be swarming all over that atelier before morning. That was my feeling, anyway. Phoebe turned from the window. A car was arriving. I locked the door and pushed the key back through the mail-flap. The chauffeur was a middle-aged man in grey livery and wearing dark glasses. I told him to take us to the Faculte des Sciences. Ilinka lived on a tiny square not far from the Jardin des Plantes. When the wind blows from the west you can hear the animals in the zoo. The snow was driving in from the north, chased by a buffeting wind, thickening the window-ledges, coating the umbrellas of the last stragglers making their way home. It was no night for a dog to be out on the streets, let alone a man on the run. The outline of the massive granite building loomed ahead and the chauffeur cut his motor. He touched the peak of his cap but said nothing.

'Wait here,' I told Brown and took his sister's arm. We walked close like lovers, our footsteps deadened by the snow on the ground. We hurried past the convent wall and into the Place des Religieuses. Five small houses enclose a fountain where white marble dolphins spout water into a basin. The whole square is no bigger than a regulation-size tennis court. Four of the houses are used as offices by a couple of firms of architects. At night they are empty. Ilinka's house is the fifth, tucked away in the righthand corner with a street-door that opens directly on to the narrow pavement. There's a garden behind it with chestnut trees and an iron door that opens into the convent grounds. It's usually locked and camouflaged with ivy but Ilinka has a key. The Mother Superior is an Hungarian and an old friend. Summer evenings, Ilinka slips into the garden and crochets with the nuns. Two lamps lit the square, silent under its white cover, Ilinka's drawing-room has the only windows on the front at street-level. I tapped softly on the pane. The doorbolts were withdrawn immediately and warmth flooded out of the hallway.

Ilinka was wearing a red velvet dress with a lace bodice and cuffs and an apron. Women tell me that there is no such thing in this age as silk stockings. I can only report that Ilinka Ostrava has them by the dozen, still packed in the boxes of long forgotten Buda-Pesth hosiers. Her white hair was piled high on her head. Her face is wrinkled but the bone-structure is so good that you're not really aware of the wrinkles. Her eyes are as black as her hair is white and a graphic guide to whatever she happens to be thinking. It makes her a bad liar. She snap-shotted Phoebe with one quick look and fastened an arm round the girl's shoulders.

'In with you quickly by the fire, off now!' Her eyebrows were question marks to me.

I closed the street-door. 'Are you sure that driver's all right? It's possible that the police make a check of all the car-hire firms.'

'Bah!' The way she says it, the word is expressive. 'Nikolai Leschinsky knows what to do.'

I could smell coffee brewing in the kitchen and firelight danced in the drawing-room.

'I have to go,' I said regretfully. 'Could I borrow your car in the morning? If it's blown up I'll replace it.'

She frowned. 'Blown up?'

I waved a hand. 'A joke.'

Phoebe was standing in front of the fireplace. 'I don't know where you found this man, my dear,' said Ilinka. 'But beware of him. He is completely unscrupulous.' She smiled brilliantly, putting the girl at ease.

'Do I get the car or not?' I asked.

She indicated a silver dish on a sidetable. I picked up

the ignition-keys and put them in the pocket of my anorak.

'It is sitting in the garage by Place Monge,' said Ilinka. 'I will tell them that you are coming.'

I nodded good night to Phoebe, my voice low as Ilinka came out to the hallway.

'Don't let her out of the house. I'll tell you everything in the morning.'

She touched my cheek and shut the door on me. The motor was running when I climbed in the back with Brown. I told the driver where to go.

'She's in good hands,' I said to Brown. I had the feeling that he was much happier now that the initiative had been passed to someone else. The mackinaw made him stand out like a Michigan duck-hunter and I knew I'd have to do something about it. It was almost two in the morning when I paid off our driver. I gave him twice the amount that he asked for. He took off his cap, bowed low and drove off. We were outside the hotel yard. The door was open so that the garbage collectors could pick up the trash in the morning. I shoved Brown through and made him crouch down behind the loading-platform. He looked about as happy as a bishop in a whorehouse. Somebody emptied a bath overhead and hot scented water spilled over the drain. I walked round to the front of the hotel. Three cars were parked outside, George's Cadillac and a couple of nondescript vehicles. The whole square was in darkness except for the light from the hotel portico. I went in behind the revolving doors. Mikhail had gone home. The only person on duty was the night-porter, an old man who just about manages to creep from one year to the next. He was sitting on a chair under a hot-air duct. The bar was still open. George was at the same table, rapping with friends. I waved to him, collected my room-key from the desk and walked down the passage towards the elevator. I slammed the gates hard and ducked through the pass-door leading to the kitchen. The sound of the voices in the bar filtered out to the kitchen. I unlocked the yard-door. A flurry of snow drove into my face. Brown came from behind the loading-platform, one hand hanging on to his spectacles. I pulled him on to the service-stairs, shut the door to the yard and found a cloth. I dried out the stone-flags where our footsteps showed. George always makes a tour of the premises before going to bed.

I shepherded the nervous Brown upstairs. He wasn't too sure what was going on, which was fair enough. I wasn't too sure myself at that moment. I opened my room and threw him my robe and a towel.

'Your bed's the one farthest from the window. Take a bath.'

I raised the porter and gave him Misty's London number. He repeated it, wheezing like a leaky bellows. The number rang for some time before Misty's sleepy voice came on the line.

'Yes, who is it?'

'Don't tell me there's someone else who calls you at half-after two in the morning,' I retorted.

The bed creaked. 'Just a minute, let me light a cigarette.'

'I'm on to something really big,' I said. 'Big and possibly dangerous.'

'Male or female?' she asked.

I gripped the phone very tightly. 'We'll dispense with the snappy dialogue. You'll find a message waiting at the office: ignore it. I *won't* be back tomorrow – got it?'

There was no answer. 'Are you listening to me, goddammit?' I half-shouted.

'Don't swear at me,' she said primly. 'You won't be back tomorrow. It's a pity, because I miss you.'

'Me too,' I said. 'Find out how long the police can hold a suspect in France without charging him actually. Ring their Embassy or something.'

'I can tell you that without getting out of bed.'

I recognised the tone. If Misty says she knows, she knows. 'O.K.,' I said. 'Tell me.'

The bed creaked again. I could almost smell the Turkish tobacco she uses and wished I was there beside her.

'It isn't the police who decide,' she informed me. 'It's the Examining Magistrate. He's the one who says when and if a charge is brought. It all depends how long he takes to make up his mind. This girl waited more than a year.'

It was nearly three o'clock in the morning. 'Which girl?' I asked patiently.

'This girl I was at school with, Angela Baird. She shot a ski-instructor in Chamonix. He's got a wooden leg now. Next question.'

'Just don't get fresh,' I warned. 'Remember the respect. I need the name of a good criminal lawyer here in Paris. Name, address and telephone number. Could you get that by ten tomorrow morning, do you think?'

'For love I'll do anything,' she replied. 'I'll call you at the hotel. Where are you speaking from, incidentally?'

'The hotel,' I said.

'I thought it might be a jail. You haven't robbed a bank or anything – or strangled Ilinka?' The last was on a hopeful note. God knows why an attractive chick of twenty-five bothers to be jealous of an old lady, but this one did.

'Here comes the schlock,' I said. 'Tell Baxter I want a thousand pounds payable at the First National Bank, Rue de Rivoli, first thing in the morning.'

She whistled like a boy. 'A thousand pounds! I can hear him now, screaming all the way down to the ambulance. You can't be serious!'

'Never more so,' I said. 'Tell him he can hold me personally responsible for the money – attack my pay – anything. But I need that bread. Good night, baby. Keep everything warm for me.'

Her voice was only just audible. '*When* are you coming home? I really do miss you.'

'A couple of days,' I said. 'And you'll be proud of me.' I blew a kiss into the mouthpiece and hung up.

The curtain changed pattern as the portico light outside was extinguished. George was on his rounds. Brown came out of the bathroom, wearing the bath-towel like a toga.

'I thought I heard voices,' he said, peering round as if expecting to find someone under the bed.

'You did,' I answered. 'I was on the phone.'

I switched on the radio while I was brushing my teeth. The weather forecast promised more snow with below zero temperatures. Brown was in bed when I left the bathroom. I cut the light.

'What exactly did you have in mind when you went over the wall this morning? What could you possibly hope to gain? Crissakes, you didn't even have a bed to go to!'

He moved around restlessly. 'The only thing on my mind was to beat that wall. The rest would be easy.

When you live with something night and day, you're not being exactly rational. I realised the truth though, the moment the car broke down. But I still had to go on.'

'Go on where?'

'God knows,' he answered. 'I used to dream of stepping through Carnot's bedroom window and forcing him to speak the truth.'

'Was that the reason for the gun?'

He didn't answer. The lights of a passing car lit the ceiling. His eyes were closed.

'You realise that it's not just you,' I added. 'You've dragged your sister into it.'

His voice was obstinate. 'I don't think we need outside advice about anything we do for one another.'

I pounded a hole in the pillow. 'Sure. You people don't need anything or anybody. All you need is a miracle.'

I could hear his heavy breathing in the darkness. 'How do we get her out of it, Macintyre?'

'With any sort of luck she comes out with you,' I said. 'I'll have the name of the best lawyer in Paris by ten o'clock.'

He made a sound in his throat. 'What makes you think that he'll believe me. Nobody else has.'

'There's me,' I pointed out. 'And we'll get him the proof. Forget Carnot for the time being. You don't land sharks with trout-bait. Let's get some sleep.'

It was still dark when I woke. Brown was lying on his side, head under the covers, one arm trailing. I shaved, dressed and touched him on the shoulder. He rolled over, coming up blindly in a defensive position. I gave him his spectacles.

'It's almost nine o'clock. I have to go out for a moment. I'm going to leave you locked in.'

He swung his feet to the floor and knuckled through his crewcut. 'I'll be all right,' he yawned. 'God, I'm hungry. The last time I ate was yesterday morning.'

I pulled the curtains back. The weather forecast was on the button. Long icicles dangled from the guttering, last night's snow was covered with a frozen crust and a pale sun hung in a cloudless sky. It was country weather and all it did for the city was show up the dirt.

I bundled his shirt and pants inside the mackinaw and put them under my arm.

'If the phone rings,' I said from the door, 'don't answer.'

The corridor was like a tomb. No noise of any kind is allowed before ten. I went down the service-stairs to the kitchen. The maids were drinking coffee. I ordered a couple of boiled eggs for breakfast and pushed open the pass-door. The only person in the lobby was the old watchman, bleary-eyed and sprouting a grizzled stubble. The cold on the street stiffened the hairs in my nostrils and my feet rang on an iron-hard pavement. But the sweater and golf-jacket kept my body warm. People I passed on their way to work were muffled to the eyeballs. Furs, wraps, scarves and ear-muffs. Only the young girls braved the weather in mini-skirts and boots. The department-store on the corner of the boulevard had just opened. I badgered a still dozey clerk into selling me a suit that would fit Brown and added a topcoat for good measure. I'd get it all back on expenses and I wanted him to look the part for the pictures I had in mind. It was well after nine by the time I collected Ilinka's little Renault. I stopped on the way back to the hotel and donated Brown's old clothing to a Salvation Army post.

Mikhail had come on duty. I told him about the call I expected from Misty, collected my breakfast-tray from the kitchen and carried it upstairs. George's staff is well-trained. Nobody passed any comment. I put the tray on the floor and stuck the key in the lock. Brown had shaved and looked as if the night's rest had done him good. I chucked the package of clothing on his bed.

'Try those for size.'

The suit was made of stiff grey tweed with a square-cut jacket and wide lapels. With his brush-top head and spectacles Brown could easily have passed as a teacher from an Ecole Polytechnique. A maths teacher, maybe, who played a little mild tennis at the weekend.

'You'll do,' I said. 'If they ever get real close to you it won't matter what you're wearing. Help yourself to coffee.' I got myself a mug from the bathroom and let Brown eat the eggs. He went through the croissants. washing them down with cups of the good Salvadorean Highland brew. When he'd done, he stacked the plates on the tray and put it by the door. Like me he had the habits of the bachelor. He gestured at the transistor.

'I listened to the news while you were out. Don't worry, I kept the volume down.'

I sat by the phone. It was almost ten o'clock and Misty keeps railroad time.

'Do tell,' I said. 'The ports are being watched and an arrest is imminent?'

He shook his head, 'There wasn't a single word about me. Not one single word.'

I leaned back against the bedhead. 'So much the better. That means that you're yesterday's news.' It didn't mean anything of the sort, of course, but there was no reason for him to know it.

The phone rang. It was Misty and she was already at the office. I could hear the teleprinters clattering in the background.

'Do you have pencil and paper?' she asked.

I block-lettered the name and address that she gave me, looking at it doubtfully.

'Are you sure that's right, Misty? Avenue Victor Hugo?'

Her voice was tart. 'Of course it's right. Why?'

'I don't know,' I said. 'It just sounds a bit unlikely for a mouthpiece, that's all.'

'You asked for the best, not the most predictable,' she snapped. 'I left Baxter a couple of minutes ago. He's okayed five hundred pounds.'

It was half what I'd asked for but more than I had expected. 'What did he do, insure my life or something?'

'He's regretting it already,' she said. 'The transfer went by telex. It ought to be there by now. I wish to God you'd tell me what you're up to, Ross. If only to deal with Baxter. He's about to work himself into a tantrum.'

'Keep him off my back,' I warned. 'Tell him I've gone to see Picasso or something. And listen, the moment you leave that office you're to go straight home and stay there, hear? And tomorrow and the next day, all month if necessary. Do you hear what I'm saying?'

'I hear,' she said distantly. 'I'll start knitting a bed-jacket for you. Good-*bye*!'

I put the phone down and asked Mikhail to call Susini's number. His secretary came on the line. I gave her my name and asked for an appointment. In an hour's time if possible. It turned out that a lawyer's book is as crammed as a dentists. She offered me fifteen minutes and eleven-forty-five. I took it. Brown was watching me from a chair across the room.

'The lawyer,' I said unnecessarily, hauling myself to my feet. 'How does John Wayne grab you?'

'John Wayne?' he puzzled. 'I don't get it.'

'They'll want to clean the room,' I explained. 'You can't stay here and you can't roam the streets. For the time being at least it's the movies. There's a continuous show uptown that starts at eleven.'

I was combing my hair at the mirror. I blew the short-back-and-sides scene over a year ago. Everyone except maybe Baxter seems to like the result. I could see Brown, his face diffident as he spoke.

'Is there no chance of speaking to Phoebe?'

'Absolutely none. It's a little late to start worrying about her, isn't it?' I turned away from the mirror.

His face reddened. 'You appear to get a big bang out of putting people down. Is that right, Macintyre?'

I tapped the middle of my forehead. 'Wrong. I just don't like kitsch. Your sister's on the run because of you, not because of me. Help me make this bed.'

We tidied up the room and I checked the bathroom, making sure there were no signs of double occupancy. I had to get him out of the hotel before George was about. Since the maids were already on the premises it would have to be through the front. Luck was with us. Mikhail walked out to the kitchen as we stepped from the elevator. I hustled Brown across the pavement and into the beatup green Renault. Ilinka has a theory about cars that accounts for the appearance of her own. Nothing that happens to the exterior, she claims, is worth repairing. I backed the Renault, peering up at George's windows. His curtains were still drawn. Brown took yet another of my cigarettes. I remembered that when I had emptied his pockets there had been no money in them. It seemed that whatever cash they had, Phoebe was holding it. Brown didn't understand that he'd broken about every rule in the Escapers Handbook. Apparently he thought it was quite natural, as if he had a magic wand or something. I gave him a couple of bills and some change.

It was the first time I had ever seen Paris completely under snow. Rooftops glittered under the wintry sun and there were scabs of ice in the sheltered places. Salt had been sprinkled on the streets but traffic went at the same furious pace. Nothing phases the French driver. The Renault came out of the swirl at the Rond-Point as if it was on rails. If you enter Champs-Elysees in the wrong lane you stay there. The lights were burning in the *Post* bureau as we passed underneath. My feeling was that Baxter would be calling Paris any time now and telling Longman to check on me. We left the car on the slip-road and crossed to the east side of the thoroughfare. It could have been my imagination but there seemed to me to be an unusual number of cops around. I kept Brown talking to take his mind off them but he hadn't noticed. Maybe because he'd taken off his spectacles and was walking shortsightedly. We found a delicatessen on Rue de Berri. The counterman put up some chopped liver sandwiches for Brown and we walked into the nearby movie-theatre. The show had just started. We found seats at the back, immediately underneath the projectionist's booth. I could see Brown's face. He was wearing his spectacles again.

'I'm splitting,' I said. 'You know what to do?'

He took the unlit cigarette out of his mouth. 'Stay here till you come back. If you're not back by six, I take a cab to Gunn's and wait in the bar. No matter who speaks to me, whatever they say, I don't speak the language.'

I nodded and walked down the aisle towards the lavatories. There was no-one to see me lift the bar on the emergency exit. I stepped out into the alleyway, rounded the block and hurried north. Twelve avenues converge at Place Charles de Gaulle like spokes round a hub. Susini's address was a house facing the Arc de Triomphe. A forbidding iron door was set in a brick wall that followed the curve of the pavement. I pressed the only bell in sight and the door opened. A path had been swept in the snow as far as the steps. I climbed up and cleaned my shoes on a scraper. Rows of brass plates advertised various commercial undertakings. The plate at the bottom simply said SUSINI. I let myself into a carpeted hallway where a uniformed concierge directed me to the right. The secretary in the reception-office finished her telephone conversation, one eye on the clock. I was three minutes late.

'Maitre Susini is waiting,' she said severely and ushered me into another room.

There was a complete hush the moment I shut the door behind me. Not a sound penetrated the four big windows that faced the street. Never in my life had I been in a lawyer's office like this one. Ornate gilt rings and scrolls embellished the heavy furniture and stuffed birds hung on the walls, birds of prey. Hawks, owls and an evil-eyed eagle holding a miserable-looking rabbit in its talons. The only compromise with Susini's profession was the desk he was sitting behind. He came to his feet easily, not unlike a heron himself, elegantly clad in a blue suit and a stiff winged collar. He had little hair and gave an impression of something feline when he moved.

'Vous parlez francais, Monsieur Macintyre?'

I took the chair he indicated. 'Not as well as you speak English, I suspect. Very few foreigners manage to get my name right first time round.'

He put his head back and laughed like an actor, photographing me with his eyes all the while.

'I had four years at Harvard Law School. Have a cigarette and tell me what I can do for you.'

I opened a box on the desk that was embedded with chunks of emerald-matrix.

'That's really the whole point, Maitre. You see I'm not here for myself. I'm an agent for someone in trouble.'

He displayed his teeth confidently. The bridge-work was magnificent. 'I specialise in criminal cases, Monsieur Macintyre. Those who come to me for advice always *are* in trouble.'

'This is very basic trouble,' I said.

He dismissed the phrase with a wave of his hand. 'Basic problems are the easiest to dispose of. Are you at liberty to discuss the nature of your principal's difficulty?'

I liked his style, the way he put his words together. He was a long way removed from the cigar-chomping bums I'd known in Montreal.

'Yes and no,' I answered. 'There's a good reason for me being vague. My friend is facing a very serious charge. And for the moment at least he's unable to support his defence with fact.'

'Ah bon,' he said quickly. 'Perhaps we should consider his position as it stands, then.'

For many reasons, including some that I couldn't yet define, I felt this was my man.

'There's a warrant out for my friend's arrest,' I said flatly. 'But he doesn't intend to give himself up without trying to establish his innocence. I happen to believe in him, that's why I'm helping. What we want from you would come later. We've given ourselves a time-limit. When that's elapsed I'm going to bring him in here and ask you to surrender him to the authorities.'

He leaned back in the padded leather chair, tracing the outline of an eyebrow with a forefinger.

'Exactly how much do you know about law, M. Macintyre? French law, British law, *any* law, in fact?'

I looked away from the glassy glare of the eagle. 'Very little, I guess. You mean I'm compounding a felony or something?'

Half-shut eyes considered what I had said. 'Whatever you tell me here is privileged. I was thinking about this friend of yours. The longer he is at large, the more difficult the ultimate explanation. However there is another aspect. Assume two men are together in a lonely place and one of them accidentally kills the other. The killer panics and runs. The law requires him to surrender, to make his submission to the body corporate. A cynic might remark that this is not the nature of innocence, but it *is* the law.'

'I'm with you so far,' I said. His cigarettes were my own brand.

'Good,' he answered. 'Now suppose shock has robbed the man of the power to think rationally. This would be a justification of his conduct, backed by medical evidence, of course.'

I saw where he was taking me. 'That's out,' I said firmly. 'There's no question here of insanity. We've got a conspiracy on our hands. A frame-up with every witness lying his head off.'

His fingers were like butterflies, touching, alighting, never still. 'What do you do for a living, M. Macintyre?'

'I'm a writer,' I said.

His smile came and went. 'I imagined something of the sort. You chose me as a sort of guard-dog, is that it?'

'I was told you were one of the best criminal lawyers in Paris.'

He opened and shut a drawer. 'The *best,* M. Macintyre. I'm also a very bad loser. And what you are asking me to do is defend an unknown individual who is about to be charged with an unspecified offence. This seems to me to be suspiciously like loading the dice against oneself.'

I rose. 'I'm sorry I wasted your time, Maitre.'

He moved round the desk and put himself between me and the door.

'If your friend has six thousand francs I will act for him. Half payable now, the rest when his problems are resolved.'

I touched my pocket. 'I don't have that sort of money with me. I can get it though in half-an-hour.'

'Perfect,' he said and scribbled on a slip of paper. Like an actor again he was able to turn on the charm quickly and convincingly.

'My private telephone number. If you should need me out of hours they'll tell you where to reach me. By the way, the Police Judiciaire know me well. Tell your friend it would be advisable to mention my name as quickly as possible. If necessary, of course.' His smile was brilliant.

I had an odd feeling that he suspected that I was the culprit. 'I'll tell him,' I promised. 'Thanks.'

'Enchanted,' he said and opened the door. 'Mlle Descartes, tell M. Macintyre how he can make a money transfer. Good day, Monsieur.'

My next call was at the bank. Baxter's transfer was through. I identified myself, sent Susini's fee on its way and drew the balance in cash. It was almost one o'clock. An east wind was freezing the slush in the gutters. It didn't really matter where or what I ate. I settled for an automat at the bottom of Avenue de l'Opera. The pared-down menu was aimed at budget-travellers but there was plenty of room and the food was edible. I carried a bowl of chile to a table and quenched the ensuing fire in my stomach with a glass of French beer. That done, I smoked a cigarette and bought a slug for the phone. Ilinka had held my hand too many times in the dark not to be completely trusted.

'Are you alone?' I asked. She said that she was. The girl was still sleeping. 'Keep her in the house,' I cautioned. 'If she as much as puts her nose outside she'll spend the next couple of years in jail.'

Ilinka made a sound of exasperation. 'Telephone calls in the middle of the night, tapping on the windows. When do you intend to tell *me* what is going on?'

'Just as soon as I possibly can,' I soothed. 'But not now. Here's something to occupy your mind. Find out anything you can about a man called Paul Carnot. He's in charge of security at U.N.S.C.A.D.'

'U.N.S.C.A.D?' she repeated sharply. Her mistrust of

international organisations goes back to the old League of Nations. 'What do they want with security?'

'I don't know,' I said patiently. 'Nor do I care. It's beside the point anyway. I want to know what your colonels think about him. His background, where he comes from. And do it carefully. We can't afford to put him on his guard.'

'You do your work and I shall do mine,' she retorted. 'When am I going to see you?'

I checked my watch. 'I can't give you a definite time. As soon as I can make it.'

The usual scruffy-looking bunch of self-styled students was hanging round the entrance to the Paramount. I never understand why these kids put the military down and still ape their uniforms down to the shoulder-flashes. As a send-up it's pathetic. Most of them looked spaced-out and all were peddling something or other. Charter-flight seats, pot, copies of the *Herald-Tribune*. Monday's always a big day around a travel agency. A guy with a strained smile and a drip-dry suit was rounding up a bunch of blue-rinsed matrons in stone-coloured raincoats. A steady stream of money was going over the counter in exchange for travel-vouchers, theatre-tickets, twelve different ways of seeing Paris by night.

I went downstairs to the mail-counter. They've cleaned the place up this last couple of years. The bums have gone. There are no more of those operators from Bent Barrel, Michigan dropping their rosary beads for you to pick up. What's left are the troubled in spirit, the anxious-faced travellers waiting for the letter that never seems to arrive. I showed my passport to a plump girl with moles on her throat. She riffed through a stack of letters and shook her head.

'Nothing for you today, Mr Macintyre. I'm afraid. You could try this afternoon if you like. There's another delivery round about four o'clock.'

There was nobody else at our end of the counter, and her manner encouraged me. I rested an elbow and lighted a cigarette.

'There's no hurry. Tomorrow, the next day. Tell me, were you here in August?'

She was putting the letters away, her back to me. 'I've been here since January last year.'

She turned round and I opened my fist on my press-card. 'I'm trying to trace a guy who worked here. He left suddenly in August.'

'*Are* you?' she said, and the friendliness had gone from her voice.

I put the card away. 'Did I say the wrong thing?'

She could have left but she stood her ground, having a little trouble controlling her hands.

'Let me get this right. Do I understand you to say that you're a newspaperman and you're looking for Bob Hendrikson?'

I nodded. 'That's right. If you're a friend of his tell him there's a nice piece of change coming his way with no hang-ups attached. Tell him everything he says will be in the strictest confidence.'

'He'd appreciate that,' she said in a small tight voice. Without the friendliness she was a brown-haired overweight woman with blemishes.

An old flame, I thought. A summer affair. I gave her what I hoped was the right sort of smile.

'Then maybe you'd give me his address, I could tell him myself.'

'Of course,' she said. 'You'll find him in the eighteenth

arondissement, Rue Elex. You can't miss it. It's the cemetery.' She stuffed a handkerchief into her face and fled.

I got out of there as quickly as possible. I could have seen the manager, I guess, but whoever had framed Brown had put the contract out on Hendrikson. I was sure of it and the answers weren't going to come from some fatassed Rotarian. I walked down Avenue de l'Opera to the garage and gave the parking-jock my ticket. I called the United States Consulate-General while he was getting the Renault. The girl at the switchboard passed me on to someone with a bad case of mumbles. No sir, he was afraid information of that nature wasn't divulged to strangers over the telephone.

I caught him before he hung up. 'The name is Macintyre of the London *Post*. Check it out with your public relations people.'

He used another line, shifted the marbles in his mouth and gave me the information grudgingly.

'Mr Hendrikson's death was due to gunshot wounds. The next-of-kin have been informed and the matter is in the hands of the local authority.'

I walked out to the beatup Renault, wedged myself behind the small wheel and drove across town. The tenants in Place des Religieuses have the right to park behind the west convent wall. The architects cars were already there, a couple of D.S.21's, identical in year, model and colour. The square is quiet even in the daytime, quiet enough to hear the starlings quarrelling on the roofs. The dolphins spouted icicles into the fountain and the basin was frozen over. The street-door was open. Ilinka must have seen me coming. I closed it, hearing her voice upstairs. I went into the drawing-room. The houses on the square were originally appendages to the convent. Ilinka's was the laundry. It has two bedrooms and a bathroom on the second floor, a drawing-room, study and kitchen below. Perfect proportions create an illusion of space.

Jan Ostrava never made much money from his writing. Few political emigres with right-wing sympathies ever do. *The Arts Under the Sickle* took him six years to write. A clinically-objective analysis of the decline of culture in Eastern Europe it sold two thousand and six copies. Most of them went to schools and universities where the book was discussed as an example of reactionary thinking. Ilinka had always been the breadwinner. At twenty years of age she had run away from an unbelievably aristocratic home to marry a history-teacher. In five years she learned more about the legend of documentary movie-making than the rest of the so-called experts put together. By the time she was thirty, Ilinka had become Madame Cinematheque, the ultimate authority on the early days of the industry, honoured chairwoman at film conventions and a life-pensioner of the Modern Museum of Art.

An old-fashioned fire was burning in the grate, the chintz on the chairs and sofa matched the curtains. I love the house dearly but there are certain things in it that nothing and no-one can make me appreciate. The Aubusson carpets, for instance. I've never seen an Aubusson that didn't look as if it had come from the town trash-heap. That goes for some of the paintings. I like the Paul Klee, principally because it was a gift from the artist and a mark of the esteem cultured people had for the Ostravas. The oak floors are two hundred and fifty years old and they creak. Somebody was moving around in the room overhead. I sat down near the fire and lit a cigarette. Ilinka's little black book was next to the phone along with her pearl-handled pistol. The book is usually kept in the study safe with the garnet-and-jet set and chunks of semi-precious stone that Ilinka calls her Crown Jewels. There are numbers listed in that book that are virtually unobtainable to other people, certainly to someone like me. I've seen her using it, composing numbers that linked her with closed telephone-circuits and put her through to ministry exchanges. I heard her voice and pitched my smoke into the fire. Ilinka was waiting at the head of the stairs dressed in a 1940 Chanel suit, her white hair tied back with a ribbon. Nobody else would have gotten away with it. I put my lips against her soft old cheek.

'Love you.'

'Hah! Then you have something to hide,' she retorted, her black eyes lively. She pushed me in front of her into the bedroom.

Phoebe Brown was sitting up in the fourposter, a silk crocheted scarf round her shoulders. I recognised the scarf as one of Ilinka's. There were magazines by the bedside and a bowl of freesias.

I wiggled my fingers at her. It was well after two by the clock on the mantel.

'Sleep well?'

The soft light from the bracket-lamps gave her hair the colour of a lion's mane. The smudges of fatigue had gone from beneath her eyes. She looked a different woman.

'Like a log,' she said lazily.

I tried to ignore the smile that passed between them and assumed a show of heartiness.

'Well, that's great. You're going to have to excuse us for a while. I have to talk to Ilinka.'

Ilinka was leaning against the wall like a teenage hoyden. 'There is no need, mon choux. She has told me everything.'

I looked from one to the other. 'Bully for you. Then I'll go downstairs. One of you can tell me when I'm wanted.' It was logical enough. I'd brought the girl to the house and women confide in one another. Nevertheless the sudden intimacy rankled.

Ilinka came off the wall, shaking a finger at me. 'Stop it this minute and give me a light!'

I should have known better than to throw my own cigarette away. Ilinka smokes anywhere, on the street if she feels like it, for all I know in church. She fitted a cigarette in her long tortoiseshell holder and bent her head over the flame. She gave two puffs and went into a ridiculous smirk.

'The girl says that she is not your mistress.'

I glanced across at the bed. Phoebe smiled and closed her eyes.

'Thank you, Ilinka,' I said. 'I'm grateful for your delicate approach.'

'Merde,' she said and blew a stream of smoke into my face. 'And the brother you do not know, so what exactly are you up to?'

I loosened the neck of my sweater. 'I'm trying to earn a living that's all. And at the same time right an injustice if you'll pardon the expression. Let's get one fact established while we're about it. These people involved me in their caper. It wasn't the other way round.'

Phoebe Brown opened her eyes again. 'I already told you that. It's true.'

Ilinka patted the end of the bed vaguely. 'Of course it's true, dear. I'm trying to find out if you young people know what you are doing.'

'*I* know what I'm doing,' I told her. 'How about you, you old busybody?'

Her smile slid away, her eyes self-satisfied. 'You asked me to find out about this Carnot. The thing that makes it all interesting is what I *cannot* find out.'

'Riddles,' I said sarcastically. 'That's all I need. What happened, did your colonels mutiny?'

She made a gesture of supreme contempt. 'This is not England, mon choux. Nor is it your precious Canada. M. Carnot is being protected by someone in high places. There is a big wall around him at the present moment.'

'Maybe it's not as big as you think,' I suggested. 'Do you remember a piece in the newspapers a few months ago about S.D.E.C.E. being mixed up in drug-running?'

She turned her mouth down. 'Of course I remember it. So will my butcher. I will tell you what he said. "A dastardly attempt by the Americans to discredit the French Secret Service." '

'You mean your *butcher* talks like that?' I demanded.

'Why not?' she answered composedly. 'This is France. In any case you are barking in the wrong tree, mon ami. It is the Union Corse that controls drug-smuggling not S.D.E.C.E.'

'I didn't say "Control",' I argued. 'I said "mixed up in". Did you find out anything at all?'

She waved her cigarette-holder airily. 'A great deal. This chemist, for instance. Bernanos. Six months before he died he bought a *mas* in the Var, an isolated farm-house surrounded by two hundred hectares of olive-trees on the road to Mons. He paid cash and told the real-estate agent in Draguignan that he would be retiring there soon to write a book. Does that give you any ideas?'

I was determined not to show my surprise. 'Sure. He'd been operating almost two years at U.N.S.C.A.D. and it was time to move on. These people never run a thing into the ground. The farmhouse would have been his next lab. But they killed him first. I guess he got greedy. Someone else got himself killed. Hendrikson.'

Phoebe's face was blank. 'The mail-clerk at Paramount,' I explained.

Ilinka's gesture scattered ash over the carpet. 'He was shot in the head three times and his body was found in a boxcar on a siding in the goods station. The police report states that he was known to frequent houses of ill-repute on Rue St Denis.'

'Jesus God!' I said with feeling. 'How the hell could you know that?'

'The colonels,' she said, enjoying my discomfiture. 'They are really very clever, mon choux. The trouble is that they are hamstringed.'

'Hamstrung,' I said mechanically, glad to get a word in.

'Quiet,' she admonished. 'They are obliged to work sometimes in a vacuum, but anyway. Paul Carnot, forty-six years old, economics graduate of Grenoble University. He was trade attache in Istanbul for four years and joined U.N.S.C.A.D in 1965. He lives in modest style in Versailles with his wife, two children and a Spanish maid. Nobody knows how he came to be chosen as security chief. In fact there is nothing more about him that anyone *can* tell.'

'Can or will?' I said sourly, knowing I should have

been more gracious. We all jumped as the doorknocker fell with a loud crash. Ilinka tiptoed to the head of the staircase.

'The postman,' she said. 'I am simply saying that Carnot's dossier is not available. The official reason given is that it is "being studied by the competent authority". That means that someone is sitting on it.'

My smile was strictly from nerves. 'Well, it's a start, anyway. I've got a few ideas.'

Ilinka's eyes were suddenly sober. 'What am I going to *do* with this man! Do you believe this is some sort of game, Ross? Gangsters against the intrepid reporter?'

I could feel my face going red. 'I'll tell you what I believe. I believe in the printed word going out to millions of people, naming names, producing facts, *forcing* the authorities to do something. I've seen it at work and I know. I was never surer of anything in my whole life.'

She stroked my cheek softly, her voice tender. 'And I know you are right, mon petit. Completely right. And I am an old lady who fears for you. Would you like to hear what Guy Collard said?'

I shook my head. 'Not particularly, no. I never even heard of the guy.'

'Ah,' she said. 'But he has heard of you. Collard of the Controle des Etrangers. "Send him back to London before he gets hurt," he said.'

'He did, did he? Well let me tell *you* something. Any time you start referring to yourself as an old lady, it's the moment to duck.'

Her eyes were wary. 'All I want is for you to be careful, Ross. You don't seem to understand. These Corsicans are everywhere. They are a law unto themselves.'

I know too much about Ilinka's background, her network of friends in high places, to be astonished by the accuracy of her information. If someone with clout was protecting Carnot, it was obviously that he would know he was under suspicion.

'I've been hearing about colonels for years,' I said. 'Who saved de Gaulle's life in Algiers, who's the real boss of the Gendarmerie, who would get me off the hook if I assaulted a priest in a nightclub. The time's come for a little action. These people seem to know so much, how much do they know about the Browns?'

The girl in the bed was listening intently. 'Nothing at all,' Ilinka said calmly.

'And you haven't told them?' I challenged.

'Not a word,' she said. 'All I said was that you had a lead for a story. Officially, there is not the slightest particle of proof against Carnot.'

I shifted feet. Time was passing rapidly. 'Did you ever hear of a lawyer name of Susini?'

She was kneading the girl's feet through the bedclothes. 'Naturally. The police spit whenever his name is mentioned. He's an elegant man, a bachelor with a liking for Balmain models. His father was a close friend of the Marshal's.'

In Ilinka's house there is only one Marshal – Henri-Phillipe Petain. She has this French trick of identifying people according to their political affinities.

'Well, I just hired him,' I informed them. 'He's going to hold Brown's hand when the time comes.'

Ilinka climbed off the bed and tidied her hair in front of the glass. 'You couldn't have done better.'

'I have to go,' I said. 'I've left her brother sitting in the movies.'

Phoebe Brown looked surprised. 'The movies? What

on earth for?'

I wasn't too high on the note of criticism in her voice. 'Because it seemed to me to be the best thing to do,' I said steadily. 'In the same way I think you ought to be out of that bed and downstairs washing the crocks.'

Ilinka followed me down the stairs. 'I know how you feel but there was no need to be so rude.'

I kissed her on both cheeks. 'That kid's on the run. Somebody's got to remind her of it.'

The sun had been replaced by low, dark rolling clouds. I unlocked the Renault and ran the motor, waiting for the car to warm. I found it difficult to get the opposition in perspective. I'd been reading about the multi-million dollar drug-smuggling ring for two or three years. The C.I.A. were positive about the involvement of French secret service agents. But the Corsicans controlled the racket. I knew how they dealt with projects that became non-viable, eliminating men and material with ruthless finality. The first whiff of danger had removed Bernanos and closed down the U.N.S.C.A.D. operation. Another one would have started up somewhere else. New people would have been bribed and pressured, a new front thrown up almost contemptuously. Meanwhile, someone in high places was taking good care of Carnot. It puzzled me that with timber falling everywhere he had been left standing. He was either needed or a lot higher in the rankings than I supposed.

I backed the small car away from the wall and filtered through the side streets to Boulevard St Michel. I crossed the river and left the Renault on Champs-Elysees, in one of the slots provided for the Air France Personnel. I could see nothing in the afternoon papers about the Browns. There was a queue of about twenty women waiting outside the Rex Cinema. I walked round to the alleyway but the bar holding the emergency exit was firmly in place. I hadn't reckoned on a queue at four-thirty in the afternoon and our schedule was tight. The maids left the hotel at five and George Gunn studied his accounts. He sat at a table in the bar, worked for precisely half-an-hour and then quit. I had to get Brown into the hotel during the next thirty minutes or keep him out till much later. I walked back to the front of the theatre. Queue-jumping in France is only slightly less reprehensible than child-abduction. The women's eyes grew on stalks as I approached the ticket-office. The usherette and cashier prepared to repel the rash intruder. I bent down at the guichet, leaking distresss into my voice.

'Pardon, Madame. A friend of mine is in the theatre and he is urgently needed at home.'

She had the narrow untrustworthy head of a collie.

'The theatre is full, Monsieur. As you see, people are waiting. I cannot allow you to go in and disturb the performance.'

She might have been talking about High Mass, so reverent was her tone.

'You could have the projectionist put a message on the screen for you,' I pointed out. 'My friend's wife has just had their first child.'

She sniffed hard. 'Boy or girl?'

'A girl.' The grin I gave her must have been sickening.

She sniffed again. 'It makes no difference. Boy or girl, they all come to the same bad end.'

I blocked out a message on the paper she gave me.

COME TO THE BOX OFFICE MACINTYRE. The cashier gave the message to the usherette. A couple of minutes later, Brown pushed his way through the curtains, looking like a rabbit that has just been flushed out of a cornfield. I took him by the arm and hurried him out of the vestibule. The lights had come on the whole length of the Champs-Elysees. People on their way home were crowding into the Metro stations. We sat in the car, waiting for a chance to swing into the southbound traffic.

Brown jerked his head back at the movie-theatre. ' I couldn't believe it when I saw that message coming up on the screen. My first impulse was to run.'

'When the law gets that close to you,' I said. 'They won't be sending messages. Things are moving. I've seen the lawyer, been to the paramount and checked out your sister.'

He half-turned towards me. 'Is she all right?'

'As right as rain,' I told him. 'It must run in the family.'

'What must run in the family?'

I took my hand off the wheel, the better to explain. 'It's something to do with the way you both accept things, as if it was your right.'

His face reddened. 'I see. You mean we're not grateful enough, is that it?'

'I mean that it's not all ride,' I answered. 'You're supposed to be out there pushing part of the way.'

He was silent till we reached the Rond Point. The lights from there to the Place de la Concorde are synchronised. I revved the motor, thinking that with any luck we'd make it in one crazy free-for-all rush.

Brown came out of his hunch. 'You say you went to the travel agency?'

I took my eyes off the traffic momentarily. 'The guy you spoke to is dead. His name was Hendrikson.'

'God Almighty,' he said.

'Shot in the head three times,' I added. Gears ground and motors roared as the signals changed. The trees and lamps looked lonesome in the chilly twilight. Brown clammed up completely, chain-smoking until we reached the hotel. The bleak street was deserted. It was ten minutes after five. I pushed a finger in the direction of the kitchen yard.

'The same deal as yesterday only this time you'll go up alone. I'll give you my room-key. No matter who you see, keep your mouth shut.'

He buttoned his coat and slipped round the door into the yard. I could hear him crashing about among the garbage-cans. Luckily, no-one in any of the back rooms took notice. I drove round to the front. It was a quarter after five. George was in the bar, a panatella sticking out of his mouth like a flagpole, his account-books in front of him. There was a mound of suitcases near the reception-desk. A man wearing his hat was giving Mikhail the 'I'm from Dallas' routine. I collected my key and a couple of cables that had arrived. Once out of sight of the desk, I slipped through the pass-door into the kitchen, opened the yard and gave Brown the key to my room. By the time I'd closed the yard-door again he was halfway up the service stairs. I flushed a cistern in the men's room for Mikhail's benefit and read my cables. The first was from Misty.

SNOOPERS HERE ASKING WHO IS MACINTYRE STOP FRENCH PRESS ATTACHE RESPONSIBLE STOP ARE YOU IN TROUBLE ADVISE ME AT HOME FARRELL

The second message was briefer. WHAT THE HELL IS GOING ON BAXTER

I crumpled the two pieces of paper and dropped them in the waste-basket, smiling at George from the elevator. Brown let me into the room performing like a Warner Brothers contract-actor in a Forties gangster movie. He'd found the tin-plated gun I'd taken from him the previous night. I knocked his arm up and put the gun in my pocket.

'Get yourself a goddam slingshot,' I said.

He shut the door and stepped back awkwardly. 'I thought I heard a voice. I mean somebody else's.'

'That's all that's needed,' I said, looking round. 'You hearing voices. I have to go out. In the meantime this room's supposed to be empty. No television, no radio, no phoning. Is that clear?'

He sat on the edge of his bed, rubbing his scalp. 'How long will you be?'

'There's no way of telling,' I answered. 'There are books to read. Try to relax. I'll bring some food back for you.'

He had managed to buy cigarettes somewhere and put one in his mouth.

'I can't get that guy Hendrikson out of my mind. He came from a place called Comfort, North Dakota. He told me. Can you beat that, *Comfort*!'

'How about this girl?' I asked. 'The one you're supposed to have tried to boff. What does she look like – is she tall, short, thin or fat?'

He blew smoke at the carpet. 'She's about Phoebe's height and build. She parts her hair in the centre. Did you ever see an Irish banknote?'

I knew what he meant and nodded. 'You mean the

woman's head?'

'A ringer for Claire de Pornic,' he said. 'The face, for want of a better expression, is *pure*.' He looked at his fingernails as if surprised to find them still there.

'This place where she lives,' I asked. 'Is there anywhere I could leave a car out-of-sight?'

He hitched up his spectacles. 'There's space back-and-front. She lives at the front of the building. What do you have in mind?'

I grabbed a handful of Kleenex. My nose had started to run. 'Throw a scare into her with any luck. See which way she jumps.'

He spoke, staring down between his legs. 'I've been thinking. What happens if I turn myself in – I mean now, this very minute?' His voice sounded tired and defeated.

I crossed the room and stood over him. 'I don't have a crystal ball but I'll try guessing for you. You'd never reach the police-station alive. And while we're on the subject, let me remind you of something. It isn't just *you* any more. A whole lot of people have put themselves out on a limb for Radnor Brown, your sister included.'

He wiped his mouth with the back of his hand. 'Are you always so goddam sure of yourself, Macintyre. So certain that you're going the right way?'

'Not always,' I said. 'Just every once in a while. And this time you're going with me.'

'Yes,' he said after a moment. 'I guess so. You sure could have made a better choice.'

'There *was* no choice,' I answered. 'I told you, relax. You're the passenger.'

He pulled his feet up on the bed, making a wry face

at me. 'O.K.. I'm relaxed. Don't worry about me.'

I locked him in the room and left the key at the desk, Mikhail had gotten rid of the Texan and his baggage. I poked my head into the bar. George's panatella had burned down a couple of inches. The heating was on full-blast and he was sitting in his elegant Sulka shirt-sleeves.

'Can I have a word with you?' I said.

He cleared his throat of phlegm and put his pen down, his eyes full of suspicion.

'What the hell are you hanging around here for? I thought you were due back in London.'

I pulled a chair and made room for my elbows. 'I have my reasons. Look, George, you know some of the heavies in town. Suppose a guy wanted to reach the man at the top, how would he go about it?'

'Up yours,' he said very distinctly. 'Forget it! The deal's the same here as it is anywhere else. No organisation man is going to risk talking to a reporter. What are you looking for anyway?'

'The Union Corse,' I said. 'The Capu.'

He heaved himself out of his chair, rolled across to the door, looked out into the lobby and shut the door again. He came to rest with his back against the edge of the bar.

'Have you blown your stack or what?'

I shook my head. 'On the contrary. I have a proposition to make.'

He grunted and unrolled his shirtsleeves. He fastened the cuffs with gold clips fashioned like horses heads.

'I said forget it. There's nothing for you there.'

'A proposition that could save trouble,' I reiterated.

He rocked a little on his heels, looking at me. 'A lot of

good people use this place, Ross. They use it because they know I won't let some stupid sonofabitch bother them. O.K.? Now you run along and tend your legitimate business.'

It was the old George, the years and the fat not yet on him, dispensing rough justice in some dormitory drama. His shoes were untied, his ankles swollen the size of my forearm. I couldn't resist the question.

'Did you ever hear of a guy named Carnot?'

'Fuck you,' he said, looking like a red angry boar about to charge.

'Paul Carnot,' I amplified.

He scratched himself, still watching me all the time. 'It's a funny thing. I had it figured that you'd turned into a real sensible feller. And here you are sticking your nose in other people's woodpiles. Don't do it, kid.'

Looking at him, I realised something that had escaped me up to then.

'You really dig this scene, don't you?' I challenged. 'Mixing with mobsters, talking out the side of your mouth. When the time comes they'll probably give you a Warner Brothers funeral. White lilies, men in George Raft overcoats, the whole bit.'

His little eyes were restless. 'How many times do I have to tell you, *this is one you forget.* Do you understand my meaning, Ross. Just keep the hell out of it.'

I walked across, offering him my hand. He shifted his weight, knocked my hand up and faked a fist at my chin.

'You're a nice guy,' I said. 'And I'm not looking to spoil any single thing that you have going for you. But that's all there is to it. I still have a job to do.'

He took a deep deep breath. 'You always were a pigheaded bastard. Just don't say I didn't warn you.'

I glanced back from the door but his head was obscured by a wreath of cigar-smoke. I fished the crumpled cable-forms from the waste-basket and tore them into shreds under Mikhail's curious eyes. It was no time to be careless.

The address was near the Porte d'Auteuil. I knew the neighbourhood well enough in the summertime, the wide leafy avenues, crisp-uniformed nannies hurrying their charges towards the grass. But it was November now and night. The snow in front of the apartment-blocks was scuffed and tracked, the snowmen abandoned half-finished. The building I was looking for was a high-rise edifice on a corner site. They'd given it a pretentious name, plate-glass entrances and black-and-gilt elevators. There were a few cars parked out front. I turned the Renault on to the lot at the back of the building, cut the lights and parked by the wall. Nothing moved out there, not even a dog or a cat. Hundreds of windows stared out like watching eyes. I made my way round to the entrance. There were white walls in the lobby, tall vases with budding willow-branches. The Pornic apartment was on the first floor. I pressed the bell next to hers. The entrance door opened and a grey-haired man emerged from the apartment on my left. He crossed the lobby to meet me, the smile of welcome fading when he saw who it was.

'I'm sorry to bother you,' I said quickly. 'If I could just take a few minutes of your time. . . .'

He backed away, fending off the attack with his pince-nez. 'Non, non, Monsieur. It is a firm rule, I regret . . .'

I kept going. 'I'm not selling anything. I'm a journalist from the London *Post*. You could help us.'

He was surer of himself, standing in the doorway of

his apartment. 'The British are an island race,' he said pompously. 'They have no place in an integrated Europe.'

I shook my head. 'It's about an incident that happened outside this building last August. A woman was attacked. I'm trying to locate a witness who has not yet come forward. Someone who saw the whole thing.'

A look of extreme distaste spread across his features. 'I know nothing of any such incident, Monsieur. We are never in Paris during the summer. Good night.' He shut the door in my face, ridding himself of my presence.

I scribbled something on to the pad in my hand in the event that someone was watching. I crossed the lobby and rapped on the door of A-3. A spyhole set in the polished mahogany magnified the eyes behind it. A catch was pulled and a woman looked out through the aperture. Brown's description was accurate. Mlle de Pornic could have modelled a portrait of composed virtue. Her smooth black hair fitted her like a cap and her eyes and mouth were serene. She was wearing flat shoes and a grey double-knit suit. She fired the word at me through barely open lips.

'Oui?'

I gave her the same pitch and a quick flash of my presscard. She blocked my view deliberately as I tried to peer past her into the hallway.

'A witness who hasn't come forward?' Her voice was unnecessarily loud. I realised that she was speaking for the benefit of somebody in the room she had just left.

'That's right,' I said. 'Someone who saw the whole thing as it *really* happened.' I hadn't meant to give the word that much emphasis. The unseen listener must have had something to do with it. She slammed the door.

At the same time I heard the word 'police' spoken inside. I ran across the lobby, out of the building, away from the lights, and moved the Renault up the street. I still had a good view of the front of the Chateau Frontenac Apartments. Seconds passed and two people hurried out of A-3. Mlle de Pornic had a scarf over her hair and was wearing a good-looking fur coat. The man with her was tall with a dark overcoat. It was as much as I could see. They climbed into a mustard-coloured Fiat and skidded out of the lot. I slid down low as the Fiat gunned past. By the time I made a turn, it was out of sight. I drove fast, heading for Pont Mirabeau. I was gambling that they'd have taken Rue Molitor. I was over the bridge before I saw the Fiat again, indicators going as it changed lanes constantly. The woman was driving like a lunatic. I memorised the numbers on the licence-tags as she increased her lead. Then she veered towards the kerb without warning, spattering the sidewalk with slush. There was a taxi-stand opposite. The man scrambled out and transferred to a cab.

The manoeuvre forced a choice on me. I either followed the Fiat or the cab. I settled for Mlle de Pornic. She was travelling much more slowly as if the urgency had gone. I was a couple of cars behind when she entered a maze of narrow streets behind the Ministry of Foreign Affairs.

Suddenly my cover was gone. There was nothing between me and the Fiat.

Brake lights glowed. She stopped beneath a lamp. There were no houses on the short length of street, nothing but the blank walls of the Ministry. I could see a couple of cops standing in a nearby doorway. A bracketed sign on the wall warned that it was a one-way thoroughfare. There was no turning back and barely room enough to inch past the Fiat. Mlle de Pornic turned her head as I passed. I've never seen venom more clearly expressed in a human-being's eyes. I glanced back as I went round the corner. She was out of the car and talking to the two cops. For all I knew she was telling them I was some kind of spook who'd been following her. I put my foot down hard, expecting the blast of a whistle. Miraculously nothing happened. It took me fifteen minutes to reach Ile-de-la-Cite, another five before my brain began to control my pumping heart. I sat for a while, parked in the lee of the cathedral, telling myself I had done the right thing the wrong way. I should never have gone near the Chateau Frontenac Apartments. A phone call would have had the same effect, drawn her out of her lair. Yet I couldn't be certain. These people were pros with an instinct for danger. They had the training and equipment to deal with it. The truth was that Mlle de Pornic had taken the play away from me as neatly as a trapper skins a skunk. I was just as wise now as I'd been three-quarters of an hour ago.

I walked over to the Stepka's bistro, bought myself a brandy and asked Madame to fix some food for Brown. She came back with half-a-roast chicken wrapped in foil. It was no feast but Brown could have done a hell of a lot worse, in some stinking police-cell for instance. I made my way back to the car in a deep fit of depression. For years I've been having these sudden swings to joy or sadness, often without reason. It's either break out the champagne or a senseless walking, even in the rain. The joy is always public, the gloom nursed alone. These are what Misty calls my ambivalent periods. Doubts chased one another in the recesses of my mind. I'd done nothing about a photographer. By now Brown's story should have been on tape. And so on.

I snapped out of it, editing the account of my trip to Auteuil for the Browns. It was no time to have them losing faith in me. I hadn't looked at my watch for a while, but it must have been after seven when I parked outside the hotel. A big black Mercedes was parked next to George's Cadillac. The lights were out in my room. I pushed through the revolving doors. It was oddly quiet in the lobby. There were usually people in the bar at this hour but I could see no-one. Mikhail was staring at me from his desk, his face unnaturally pale. I glanced down, my thought that I'd tracked something in on my feet. My eyes lifted, caught by the movement on my left. The two cops I'd seen the night before in Phoebe Brown's building stepped round the bar door. They flanked me professionally, one on each side. The one with the flat ears took the chicken from my unresisting hand. He used his finger on the foil like a spear, brought his nose close to the meat and pronounced judgement.

'Excellent.' He put the chicken on the reception-desk. Mikhail seemed to have turned to stone.

George Gunn chose the moment to make his entrance, the Elder Statesman in button-down shirt and dark blue suit. He'd laced his swollen feet into his shoes. I looked at him for guidance and drew a complete blank. It was like tapping your father on the shoulder and have him turn, showing the face of a stranger.

'Excuse me,' he said, to them not to me. 'I have work to do.' He rolled across the lobby and went into the bar.

There was a noise in my ears like running water. I wasn't sure whether or not I was under arrest nor was I going to put it to the test. Whatever happened I had to keep these men from my room. I made a half-hearted gesture after George.

'If there's something you want to see me about, couldn't we talk in there?'

They smiled at one another as if I was a red-nosed comic. The flat-eared one wagged his head admiringly.

' "If there's something you want to see me about". . .' he repeated.

Suddenly we *were* in the bar with door to the lobby shut. The cops must have been here long enough to have a drink. Two empty glasses stood on the counter. George was sitting at his usual table, making a production out of lighting a panatella. One of the cops pushed a thumb hard into my right kidney.

'Hands against the wall, legs wide apart!'

You see the scene in a movie or newsreel but it has to be experienced to understand the humiliation. Fingers groped inside the neck of my sweater, felt round the waistband of my trousers. The man emptied my pockets. I'd completely forgotten the gun.

'Turn round and take off your shoes!' he instructed.

He squatted and banged each shoe hard on the floor before kicking them back at me. George was getting a ring-side view, his face veiled in cigar-smoke. The cop weighed the cheap gun in the palm of his hand.

'You have a permit for this weapon?'

His manner indicated that he wouldn't have accepted one from the Archangel Gabriel himself but I did what I could.

'I have a permit from the Metropolitan Police, yes.'

I was waiting for George to come bulling in with the magic word that would get these clowns off my back. He just sat there, his face expressionless.

The cop dropped the gun in his overcoat pocket. 'You visited an apartment in Auteuil this evening. The apartment of Mlle Claire de Pornic.'

I wiped my nose on a soggy tissue. 'That's right. I have a salary to earn.'

He leaked a mean little smile from the side of his face. 'Even if it means interfering with the due process of law and order?'

I changed the tissue for a dryer one. 'There's no law that I ever heard of anywhere that stops a guy asking questions.'

He opened his left hand. 'Is this the key to your room?'

It was an unnecessary question. He must have checked the hotel register and the room number was on the tag. George still gave me no help. I used a dry tongue on peeling lips.

'O.K. You've searched me and I'm prepared to forget it. Just don't take this thing too far.'

'Out,' said the man with flat ears. His shove sent me staggering towards the door. We made the long walk down the corridor to the elevators. There was just enough room in the cage for the three of us. One of them stuck the key in the lock and threw the door open, all in one quick continuous movement. The other found the light switch. My room was empty. There was no sign of Brown. Neither cop showed any sign of surprise. They kicked the door shut and searched my bag thoroughly. I sat on the bed watching them. Somebody had done a first-class job of tidying up. There wasn't even a cigarette-butt or match around. Suddenly it came to me that it wasn't Brown these men were interested in, they didn't even know he had been there. *Their concern was with me.* Flat ears leaned against the bathroom door and sucked a tooth reflectively.

'You have made forty-one visits to this country over the past years, Monsieur. Has anyone ever interfered with your just pursuits?'

'Those are the only kind I have.' The sally drew no response. 'Never,' I added.

'You see,' he proclaimed. 'You come and go as you please. France welcomes all those of good faith.'

'And the world is waiting for the sunrise,' I smiled. They couldn't castrate me.

He changed his feet, the image of a good fast heavyweight even stronger.

'How do I give you a warning, Monsieur?'

'That would depend,' I answered. 'You wouldn't give me one for doing my job, that's for sure.'

'Carrying a concealed weapon,' he said conversationally. 'Interfering with the course of justice, molesting a witness. We could stretch that into five or six years. Or I could use my imagination.'

I looked at each of them in turn and shook my head. 'You people didn't come here tonight worrying about a twenty-five dollar pistol.'

The cop stepped forward, lifting me up by the anorak. I felt the raw power in his arms.

'Correct, Monsieur. We came with a message. If you are not out of France by eight o'clock tomorrow morning you will be arrested.'

I brushed the fabric where he had touched me. Misty is right. It's stupidity not courage that forces me up when I should stay on the floor.

'You might not have things all your own way,' I suggested. 'I'm a Canadian citizen working for a British newspaper.'

He shoved me down on the bed again. 'Merde to your newspaper. Merde to the lot of you. Eight o'clock tomorrow morning or by the time we've finished with you, you won't be recognisable.'

The door shivered under the impact of their exit. I heard the elevator on the way down. Seconds later the Mercedes pulled away. I blew my nose again, thinking of Brown out there somewhere, running the streets like a scentless rabbit. The buzzer sounded. I lifted the house-phone. George's voice was quietly matter-of-fact.

'They've gone. Get yourself down here and bring your things with you. I'm in the bar.'

I threw the scattered clothes in my bag and left the key in the door. Mikhail started to busy himself with some papers as I stepped out of the elevator.

George was at his table, a bottle of Teacher's in front of him. The sullen look in his eyes told me that he'd been drinking.

'Shut that goddam door,' he ordered. I did as he asked. The next few minutes promised to be rough. Cigar-juice stained the corners of his mouth and his silk shirt was damp with sweat. He leaned across the table bringing his shaking forefinger close to my nose.

'Why'd you do it to me, Ross? For Chrissakes, *why*?'

The truth was of course that he was one hundred per cent right. Fat George had been left out in the dark, an ignored counsellor and a friend betrayed. I pushed his finger away.

'I'm sorry, George.'

'Sorry!' He turned his fingers into a fist and rapped it against the side of my head. 'I ought to beat on you till your brains dropped out. All these years you've been using me, conning me, and only now I see it. I lend you money, lie to your women for you, listen to those goddam novels that aren't ever going to be written. And what do I get in return – I'll tell you what – shit!'

He slopped some scotch into the glass and pushed the drink an inch in my direction. I left it where it was.

'What have you done with him, George? I have to know.'

He swirled the ice moodily. 'You see what the guy says! Not one word about me – nothing about the way I felt when the law came crashing in here. It doesn't matter that I've got friends. Suppose I didn't! The answer is that George can always take care of himself. That's the way you punks think.'

I'd seen him mad often but never like this. 'For what it's worth,' I said. 'The answer is yes. I mean yes you can take care of yourself. It seems to be more than I can do.'

He held his hand up quickly. 'Hold it!' he protested. 'Oh no, you don't hook me again! I've met some selfish bastards in my time but you're out on your own. You're way ahead of your field. Let me tell you what I thought when the fuzz walked in here tonight. I thought Ross's got in a fight. Ross got himself pulled over some woman. Ross insulted the flag. Whatever it is, nobody's going up to his room until I make sure that it's clean. By that time those jokers already had your key from the desk. So I bring them in here, tell them who I am, buy them a drink, stall them. Then I got upstairs and open your room with my pass-key. "Is that you, Macintyre?" the guy says in one of those alligator-swamp accents. And who is this guy? A punk who's just broken jail – a rape-artist whose face has been spread over every television screen in the country.'

'I have to know where he is,' I said patiently.

It was thirty years or more since he'd taken a swing at me but he was very close to it at that moment. He looked at his knuckles, shook his head, muttered and dropped his arm.

'The word's been out on you since yesterday,' he said. 'The stranger going round asking questions. The guy with the presscard. I knew my man all right from the description. Macintyre the gangbuster, the jerk! You could have had your head blown off on my premises but I protected you, kept my mouth shut. I tried to warn you earlier today but you didn't want to listen. O.K. whizzkid, you're white and over twenty-one. It's your privilege to dice with your own life. You don't have any right to mine. Bringing that bastard into my hotel was as good as putting a gun to my head.'

I knew by his face that I had crossed the line. There's no provision in George's code for an amnesty. More than anything else in the world at that moment I'd have wanted to go back in time, do things over in a different way, a way that wouldn't have involved him. I shrugged.

'You always were a lousy handicapper. Have it your own way. Do I get Brown or not?'

He scowled and my hopes took off like a lead balloon. Then a long breath released his disgust, disappointment and frustration.

'He's in the kitchen,' he said. 'Get him out of here the same way you brought him in and don't worry about the check. It's covered under the last clause in the Old Pals Act.'

He must have worked on the punchline, it came out so pat. I picked up my bag.

'So long, George. Thanks for everything.'

'Sure,' he said blinking. 'Who do you think's going to follow *your* goddam coffin – that chick in London – the old broad you see here all the time? Wise up, kid. Those were no ordinary cops. You're taking on the establishment.'

'I learned it at school,' I said. 'Along with a whole lot of other people.'

It almost got him but not quite. The scowl was back on his face.

'Have it your own way. You're the lousy handicapper not me. The cops made a note of your phone calls, by the way.'

My stomach lurched. 'How you mean, made a note? How do you make a note when the dialling system's automatic?'

'For the overseas call,' he said. 'The ones you made to London. Mikhail keeps a record of any call he makes outside the city. Wise up, Buster.'

I took myself out to the lobby. It was hard to believe that this was good-bye to George. That there'd be no more sessions up in the penthouse, rapping together. No more spring afternoons at St Cloud or Longchamps. No more mind-bending evenings spent in search of our respective fathers. I was leaving something behind that could never be replaced. Hotel clerks acquire the nose of a rat on a sinking ship and Mikhail turned his back on me. I threw a bill on the desk and shouldered the swinging baize into the kitchen. Enough light came from the bar-hatch to catch a glimmer from the copper pans. The breakfast trays were laid for the morning, mine included. Brown was waiting near the door to the yard.

'Did anyone else see you?' I asked. 'Anyone besides the

guy who came to the room?'

He shook his head. 'No.'

'We're leaving,' I said. 'Walk round to the car. I'm going out the front way.'

He nodded. 'What went wrong?'

'Nothing I care to talk about,' I said. 'At least, not now.'

The clock behind the reception-desk said five after ten as I walked through the empty lobby. The air outside smelled clean, the way freezing air always does. There were no stars, not even a whisper of wind. Just the big cold night stretching out overhead, completely black and alien. Brown hurried round the corner. I let him into the car and threw my bag on the back seat. I was confident that George knew far more than he had said. One day, maybe, hopefully, we'd let it all hang out, hear one another's side of the story. This much was certain, George would never have put me out on the street with Brown unless the police were clear of the neighbourhood. I understood the way he felt. He'd stuck his neck out for me and I'd made a horse's ass out of him. My description and passport number would be at the Paris airports by now, for all I knew throughout France. The people behind Carnot would be certain that their ultimatum wouldn't be taken lightly. They were right. Come 08 hours tomorrow morning Ross Macintyre wouldn't be found in France.

Brown lit a cigarette as I wiped my nose. His gesture bugged me for some reason.

'Can't you go five minutes without one of those things?' I demanded.

He put the pack back in his pocket. 'I heard the key in the door and thought it was you. The guy seemed to know who I was. He said the police were down in the lobby.'

'He did and they were,' I answered. 'We boobed. I'm taking you somewhere else.'

He resurrected the pack of butts, thumbed one out and blew smoke gratefully. I drove round the Place des Vosges, looking up at my window. The light was on. Gunn's Hotel had finally closed its doors on me. Brown was hunched forward, sucking in tobacco smoke as if it were oxygen.

'I went out to Auteuil tonight to see that girl,' I volunteered. 'I put my foot right in the hornet's nest. Right now they're swarming.'

'How come the police knew that I was at Gunn's?' He sounded almost indignant.

I touched the brake. 'They didn't. It was me they came for.'

He made a nervous gesture with his hand, his accent gathering Spanish moss.

'Then how come they let you go?'

'A good question,' I answered. 'They came for me but they didn't really want me. I'm just the zing-tailed fly on the moose's ass. It's the moose they're after, in other words *you*!'

He thought about this for a while, the red tip of his cigarette dangerously close to his lips.

'You mean they haven't caught on yet? They don't see the connection between Phoebe, you and me?'

I raced the motor tentatively. There was a rattle up front, somewhere near the offside wheel.

'No, they haven't. That's thanks to the fat guy who got you out of the bedroom. He used to be a good friend of mine.'

'I see.' His voice slid down the scale, subdued and apologetic. 'I'm sorry about that.'

In an odd way I enjoyed his feeling of guilt. I *wanted* him to feel responsible, anyone rather than myself.

'One more disappointment in life,' I said lightly. 'It isn't going to make that much difference. We've got the pieces, the trick is to put them together so that they work. And do it fast.'

He pitched the end of his cigarette through the window and hugged his knees.

'What did the police say to you?'

'They gave me a time-limit,' I replied. 'If I'm not out of the country by eight o'clock tomorrow morning they're going to scrape me off the walls. Or words to that effect.'

'Jesus God,' he said with feeling. 'You're leaving, of course?' His doubts and fears chased the question.

Perversity prevented me from answering him completely. 'Yes, but I can't just walk away. I've bet my professional judgement on you people. If I don't come good I'm out of a job.'

The crust of ice parted from the tyres with the sound of fine glass breaking. The car skidded and I dropped down to a lower gear. Brown was still hunched up, hands clasping his knees.

'I have to say this, Macintyre. It's your manner more than your words but I detect a kind of contempt that seems to be for us and the things we stand for. I don't really appreciate it. If it hadn't been for Phoebe I'd have told you before and taken my chances.'

The steering sent a succession of shudders up my arms to my shoulders.

'What the hell are you talking about, "taken my

chances". You did that when you went over the wall yesterday morning. You're too delicate to be on the run, my friend. What you detect is a bad case of nerves, not contempt. And try calling me Ross instead of Macintyre. It takes less time.'

He turned his head and did it but with no particular enthusiasm.

The pose reminded me of something. 'I'll have to get you in front of a camera,' I said. 'I'll bring a photographer back with me.'

We were crossing the Pont d'Austerlitz. He looked out over the water, his voice diffident.

'Does that mean that you'll be coming back too?'

'Right,' I said.

He faced me again. 'I'm getting an idea that I could be wrong about you. You put yourself down as much as you do others. You're a strange guy, Macintyre.'

I closed an eye. 'That's what I think, too.'

The streets had a hard angular brilliance. Church bells were banging messages from steeple to steeple. The lights seemed to be brighter and there were more people abroad than the day before. Derelict shapes picked over garbage in the shadows behind restaurants. Groups of youngsters hurried by on their way to the cellar discotheques. We were about half-a-mile away from Square des Religieuses. I pulled up in front of a cafe and went inside. It was hot and noisy, crammed with Negroes still grey-faced from the cold and Vietnamese with square mouths bristling with gold teeth. The sweating man behind the bar jerked his head at a booth. I could see Brown in the Renault doing his best to look inconspicuous. Any big city has its hunters and hunted where men sit in bars waiting for the hands of the clock to bring the promise of life or death. Others crouch in sleazy hotels listening for the knock on the door that must surely come. Those who haven't the means to find shelter move where the crowd is thickest, marked by the stink of their fear. I found myself wondering how much easier I'd have been in Brown's place. The wonder left me quickly as I realized I was only hours from *being* there.

Ilinka's voice answered the phone. 'Trouble,' I said, raising my voice to make myself heard. 'I'll need another bed. I'll be round in a couple of minutes.'

'Bon,' she answered and hung up. Ilinka hasn't panicked since she was three years of age.

The smell around me was that of a monkey-house. Yellow faces glistened like death masks under the low-slung lights. Only the eyes were alive. The whole room was either playing or betting on shwan-liu, a Chinese version of backgammon. Dice rattled in greasy leather cups and the occasional calls came like sounds from a jaws harp, nasal and metallic. I left a luck-coin on the bar and threaded my way through the tables, blocking my nose against the stench, and out to the street. Harsh neon lights blinked over the frozen slush. The doors had already slammed on the modest homes above, sealing the occupants in from harm for at least the next few hours. Only for those involved in the hunt there was neither place nor time for rest. I took my place behind the wheel, watching Brown struggle out of his peekaboo position. Things I'd never wanted to think about were crystallising in my mind. Fears, doubts, an understanding that I was like a man climbing a mountain-peak. It was too late to go back. I could only go up. It was either that or fall . . .

'We're going where your sister is,' I said to Brown.

'There's something I want you to remember. If this deal comes unstuck for any reason, it isn't just us who land in the shit, it's the woman who is giving us shelter. She's seventy years of age.'

'I understand,' he said, looking over his left shoulder for God only knew what.

The toughness in my voice was only partly assumed. 'I hope you do. Because this is a very special kind of person. If anything happened to her because of this caper all hell would break loose.'

A couple of youths went by, exaggeratedly slim in long leather overcoats. They peered into the car as they passed and giggled. When they walked away I could see that they were holding hands.

Brown's voice was quiet. 'Maybe this is wrong, too. But if you're trying to scare me there just isn't anything left.'

I shook my head. 'Nobody's trying to scare you. I'm simply dragging things out in the open. The house that we're going to is the safest place I know. As long as you and your sister are there I'm demanding one hundred per cent obedience.'

'You've got it,' he said readily. 'I may lack a number of qualities but gratitude isn't among them. And that goes for Phoebe.'

I swung the Renault away from the kerb, drove three blocks and left it behind the convent wall. A single stained-glass window in the chapel glowed like a great jewel. Night had closed in on the tiny square and the silence was absolute. Yellow lamplight shone on the frigid dolphins, the dirty clumps of snow. Ilinka's curtains were drawn top and bottom. The other houses were in darkness. I used my special knock, Brown standing behind me bearing his earnestness like an emblem. The door opened and I pushed him inside.

'This is Phoebe's brother,' I said, ramming the bolts home. 'Mme Ostrava.'

Thin gold bracelets rattled down her arm like curtain-rings on a rail as she extended her hand. Brown took it uncertainly then out of some dim memory bent his head and touched his lips to the liver-spotted skin. Ilinka was still wearing her square-shouldered suit. Her white hair was tied behind her ears, her reading-spectacles attached to a chain round her neck.

'How do you do,' she said to Brown. The welcome rolled through the hunting-lodge, causing Borzois to rise and turn before they settled down again. 'Have you eaten?'

'The police had his food,' I said in what was meant to be a matter-of-fact voice. 'The girl can get him something.'

Phoebe was at the top of the stairs, dressed in slacks and blouse. She was down in a flash, arms reaching out for her brother. Ilinka spoke to them quietly.

'Your brother is hungry, dear. You will find eggs and cold meats in the refrigerator. Take off your coat, Mr Brown.'

I put my cheek against hers, grateful as ever for her presence. I could hear the skillet spluttering in the kitchen already.

'Don't forget the coffee,' I called.

The fire in the drawing-room was a deep red glow. Ilinka's little black book was still by the phone but the pearl-handled pistol had been moved. I wondered how busy she had been with the book since I left. I took a seat on the sofa next to Ilinka, Brown sat opposite us.

Ilinka felt in her fringed bag for a cigarette and fitted it into the tortoiseshell holder. I just beat Brown with the light. She coiled her legs under her like a battle-scarred Siamese cat.

'Well if neither of you is going to tell me what happened, I shall have to guess. The police came to Gunn's Hotel and your fat friend hid you both.'

I passed my arm behind her shoulder. 'I'll give you a pass on that one. George hid *him*!'

Brown seemed unable to take his eyes off her. I've seen it happen a hundred times and nine times out of ten it's the men who fall. There was something almost outrageous about her vivacity, her air of knowing precisely what was necessary in all situations.

'I lost George in the process,' I added. 'Like how dare I take an escaped convict to the hotel, poke my nose into his pal's affairs, betray his confidence. He came on pretty loud and he's dead right of course. How dare *I*?'

Ilinka turned her head towards the kitchen, sniffing disapproval. 'The girl fries with oil!' Her eyes juggled Brown and then me for a second. 'How much does your fat friend know of what is happening?'

The arm behind her back was numb and I removed it. 'Will you stop referring to him as my fat friend? Anyway, how much he knows about anything is a question nobody's ever been able to answer. The safest bet is to assume that he knows *everything*. His bar is a sort of club for the Union Corse. This means that they trust him implicitly. George is well placed to hear the news. He told me earlier on, the word's been out on me since I went to Phoebe's apartment. When the police came to the hotel George didn't know Brown was in my room but he still covered up for me.'

Ash dropped on Ilinka's jacket. She brushed it away unconcernedly.

'Your speech is like your writing, Ross, elliptical. It lacks continuity. Gunn hid Mr Brown: *why*?'

I looked away. 'That's a tough one to answer, sweetie. Maybe George is a frustrated romantic. We used to look for our fathers together.'

'Ahah,' she said. 'Do something to your hair.'

I pulled it down over my ears and shrugged. 'George will never admit that Rad was on his premises. My side of the bargain is to stay out of his life from henceforth. That was the way we left things.'

'You mustn't let it matter,' she said, her eyes wise. She patted my hand. 'Did these policemen tell you where they were stationed?'

I put my chin out. 'One of them showed me a card, the first time I saw them, Quai de Bourbon. The lighting wasn't that good and I wasn't that attentive. George claims that they're something very special and they certainly acted like it. They've given me until eight o'clock tomorrow morning to get out of the country.'

'Ahah,' she said again.

I told her about it. 'I wish you'd stop saying that. You sound like Madame La Zonga, the gypsy fortune-teller.'

'Quiet,' she reproved. 'What made these men go to Gunn's? Something else must have happened since you left here.'

I took a deepth breath. 'I visited Mlle de Pornic.'

She touched the back of her hair, bracelets tinkling, her face satisfied.

'Well we know all about Mlle Pornic. She works in the Ministry of Foreign Affairs. The Middle East Division. She's a specialist in Turkish and Arabic.'

Phoebe Brown carried in a tray laden with cold cuts and celery, some kind of omelette. She placed the tray against Brown's knees. He looked at Ilinka for permission.

'Bon appetit,' she urged. 'And the coffee?'

Phoebe nodded quickly. 'I'll get it right away.' She made a second trip to the kitchen, wheeled the trolley to Ilinka's side and sat on the arm of her brother's chair. Ilinka poured and distributed the cups.

'That's very good,' I said. 'About Pornic. Very good indeed. Is there more or have we finished with the dramatic disclosure department?'

She answered in a tiny tinkling voice. 'She was stationed in Ankara at the same time as Carnot. Now for the other two witnesses. Le Commandant Kerambrun – career officer, air-attache in Teheran, Ankara and Belgrade until 1968 when he retired to grow flowers somewhere near Fontainebleau.'

She paused to wrinkle her nose again, this time so that Phoebe could see it.

'How is it that you Americans have never learned to make coffee?' she demanded.

'We think we have,' Phoebe replied, just sweetly enough. Miss Brown appeared to be losing ground fast what with cooking in oil and making a swill of the coffee. Maybe she'd set no ships alight but there was value there for those who liked the type.

I looked at my watch pointedly. 'O.K. people, let's break it up. I get the significance. They've all been to Ankara. What about the other witness?'

Ilinka was completely calm. 'You manage to sound righteous even when in the wrong. It is quite an accomplishment, mon choux.'

'A Presbyterian conscience,' I retorted. 'The other witness.'

We waited while she went through her lady-preparing-for-smoking routine.

'Pierre Pelazzi, born in Bastia, Corsica, the son of a customs inspector. I find him the most interesting of them all. He fought for the Free French in North Africa and settled in Algeria after the war. He turned up in Paris in 1960. M. Pelazzi is a *brocanteur*, a dealer in objects of small value.'

A log collapsed, showering the carpet with sparks. Brown stamped them out quickly and methodically.

'It's laudable, I guess,' I said. 'But *interesting*?'

I should have known better. She waved her cigarette-holder at me. 'What makes him interesting is the fact that he is known to have killed at least three men. Murdered them. A nightclub proprietor in Ajaccio, a moneylender in Algiers and a Turkish visitor to Marseilles.' She lowered her voice to throw the last lines away.

'That's certainly impressive,' I said. Nor was I joking. 'Do the authorities know this?'

Brown had put his tray on the floor. He had eaten very little. Ilinka mimicked my note of doubt.

'The authorities know this. But M. Pelazzi moves within the magic circle. All these people do.'

'I love you,' I volunteered. 'I only wish I were thirty years older.' I took a sip of the luke-warm coffee.

Ilinka's voice was kittenish. 'And what do *you* think of me, young man?'

Brown's face flushed. 'I didn't completely understand you, ma'am.'

Ilinka made an airy gesture. 'I am an old woman born

in the Tatra Mountains, an authority on documentary films, a diehard reactionary. I am an old woman who is forced to live vicariously, a person with access to the channels of power without the courage to tap them. Mr Macintyre did a piece on me for his newspaper some years ago. That was the gist of it.'

'Liar,' I muttered.

'Not at all,' she smiled. '"The channels of power". Ugh. Tell me, Mr Brown. First impressions have their value. I have formed mine about you, for instance. From what you observe of me do you think Ross could be right?'

I doubt that Brown had ever in his whole existence been discourteous to a woman, certainly not consciously. The movement of his adam's apple was painful to watch. The silence became unbearable. I was about to get him off the hook when he pulled himself together. The answer was a brave one.

'You're a *kind* woman, ma'am. That much I'm sure of. The rest I wouldn't know about.'

Ilinka leaned forward, swinging a silk-clad leg. 'Ah but you see, it is Ross who is right and you who are wrong.' She rose and opened the wallnut cabinet where she keeps her drink. She filled four funnel-shaped glasses with slivovitz, drained hers and passed the others round.

'To the bottom,' she ordered. We raised our glasses. 'Now,' said Ilinka, 'a plan.'

'A plan,' I nodded.

'You are going to London of course?'

'Of course,' I agreed. I saw Phoebe's violet eyes pluck question and answer from the air. 'I'll be back on the next plane,' I added. Relief flooded into the Browns' faces. Their faith in me was an embarrassment.

'I'm assuming that I'm listed at the airports,' I explained. 'My feeling is that as soon as they're sure I've left the hunt will be concentrated on this pair.'

Ilinka was unimpressed. 'You are observed leaving France. What happens to make you invisible on your return?'

Ilinka never loses battles. She simply declares them no-contests. She's also a veteran of several Iron-Curtain capers and I get a kick out of putting her on from time to time.

'Simple. The name won't be the same nor will the passport.'

She looked younger and more vital as the evening wore on. 'One does not buy passports as one buys potatoes, my friend. One needs time and connections. Time you certainly do not have. Have you the connections?'

I moved a shoulder. 'If Baxter wants the story he'll find them.'

I felt them all crowd in on me. It was the wrong thing to say. Ilinka's voice was indignant.

'You mean there is a chance that he might not want it!'

I moved to the fireplace. 'Let's not get excited. Baxter is all for the derringdo as long as there's no comeback for the *Post*. You've been in Carnot's house, haven't you, Phoebe?'

She pushed her hair out of her eyes. 'Just the once. To ask him to go see Rad.'

'What's it like?' I probed. 'Is it big, small – did you meet his family?'

'Just Carnot and the maid. It's a biggish house in the centre of Versailles. There's a garden out front with trees and shrubs.'

The fire was burning my legs and I moved back beside Ilinka. I was out of cigarettes and took one of hers.

'Let's apply reason. Rad's troubles started when he opened up that storeroom. Before that he meant nothing to these people. Imagine Carnot sitting in his hotel bedroom in Cologne. Bernanos is dead, the lab has been cleared out and the operation moved somewhere else. Suddenly this guy calls long-distance with a story about having found an envelope with photographs, records of drugs processed in the U.N.S.C.A.D. building, delivery-dates. Carnot is a pro so he keeps his cool and tells Red precisely what to do.'

Brown's expression was sardonic which was an improvement on the usual earnestness. I continued.

'Rad does what he's told. What Carnot does is anyone's guess but one thing is firmly established. If Rad *had* turned in that envelope, he wouldn't be alive and sitting in that chair.'

You sit alone, nursing the prospect of death by violence but when it's voiced by someone else it acquires fresh impact. Brown swallowed hard.

'It's ironical even to think about it. Breaking my neck to carry the news to Carnot that the good name of U.N.S.C.A.D was in danger. I *know* he believed me then. I remember his face the day he came from Germany and I repeated what I'd told him about the photographs. He looked like a terminal cancer case. Shocked and scared. If he believed me then why not now? What does he think I've *done* with the envelope? What are they trying to do to me?'

I put my empty glass on the mantel. 'Off you, as the jargon has it. Place a large-calibre pistol against your head and blow your brains out. But they won't do that till they find the envelope you've hidden.'

'Hidden?' The puzzlement under the Y.M.C.A. haircut was painful to see, an amazement that people could fail to recognise his innocence.

'That's right,' I said. 'Hidden. Here you were making fourteen grand a year, small prospects and a secret dream.'

Brown wet his mouth. 'What secret dream?'

'Everyone has a secret dream,' I said. 'You, me, Carnot. I'm trying to open his mind for you. "Extortion" he thought. "This bastard has me by the balls," he thought. When you didn't produce that letter he was certain that you'd kept it.'

Phoebe's chin came up belligerently. 'He *didn't* keep it.'

I glanced across the room at her. 'Why don't you quit being so goddam protective and listen to some sense.'

Ilinka had been tapping her cigarette-holder against her teeth. She suspended the operation.

'Someone believed that the letter went to the travel-agency. Hendrikson did not commit suicide.'

'O.K.,' I agreed. 'He didn't commit suicide. They got rid of him as we'd bat a fly. By that time somebody else was calling the plays, someone a whole lot more experienced in the game than Carnot. This guy wasn't prepared to exclude *any* possibility at all. So they got hold of Hendrikson who told them that a letter existed. He might have described it. There's nothing that sharpens the memory better than a gun stuck in the ear. But that's all Hendrikson *could* say. He couldn't say what was inside the envelope. It might have been empty, a bluff on your part.'

Phoebe took her hands from in front of her face. 'They killed that poor man for nothing.'

I nodded. 'That's what I'm trying to tell you. We've crossed the boundary into no-man's-land. The values are different. These people kill from instinct, from a sense of self-preservation. There are no moral values involved. The dead, as they say, tell no tales.'

The girl shivered. 'They're not human.'

'Right,' I said. 'Nor is this some pick-up team of hoodlums. This is the Union Corse protecting a multi-million-dollar racket. They must have agents in Hong Kong, if not they'd have flown someone there. If Rad's letter *had* reached the other Brown it would simply have been removed from him. Then the heat would have been off. But for some reason or other the letter never *has* been delivered which leaves our friends up a creek. They just can't make up their minds what Rad has done with the goodies.'

When Ilinka decides that praise is due, she fills a pail and pours. 'Ross is completely right. That is how things must have been. The escape from jail must have been the last thing these wretches wanted or expected. As long as Mr Brown was in prison it gave them time to manoeuvre. Now they have to find him quickly before he spills the bean.'

'Beans,' I said wearily. 'How much do you remember of what was in that envelope, Rad?'

His grin told me this was one question he was happy to answer. 'Practically everything.'

I gave him my pad and pencil. 'Write it all down. The order doesn't matter as long as you make it clear what you're talking about.'

Ilinka picked up the tray, fending off the girl's offer of

help. She beckoned me into the kitchen.

'I do not want you dead,' she said firmly, shutting the door.

I put the dirty plates and skillet in the sink and ran scalding water on them.

'Who's going to be dead, anyway?'

Suddenly her hands were on my arms, pinching and plucking till I had to turn and face her. Her eyes chased me into the open. There was no place to hide.

'Why are you doing this, Ross? What is driving you?'

I could hear the Browns' voices in the drawing-room, the preliminary whirring as the chapel clock prepared to strike.

'I don't know,' I said truthfully. 'To prove something, I guess. I'm no longer sure. If I blow this one Baxter's going to tear up what's left of my contract. Poaching on other people's territory, defiance of editorial policy, misuse of the newspaper's money. The only thing that will save me is the story, Ilinka.'

I was out of tissues and my nose was still running. I stuffed a length of paper-towel in my pocket.

'You spoke about a plan. Well I've got one. The Pornic woman made a fool of me but never mind. I learned a lesson, not to play from weakness. My nose tells me that Carnot's the vulnerable one and it's Carnot I'm gunning for. When I get him I'm going to need help.'

She touched the button that operated the air-extractor. The last trace of frying-oil was sucked out into the night.

'Yves Beaumarchais promised to talk to me tomorrow morning. He is my big hope but he dare not act without positive proof.'

'I'll give him all the proof he wants,' I said. 'I've been

thinking. There's only so much that you can do and I sure could use another pair of hands. I thought about bringing Misty back with me.'

The two women have only met once and that was on Ilinka's home territory. The result was a disaster. Ilinka knows that our friendship could never be in danger but the moment was embarrassing for everyone. A woman of her experience can achieve a great deal with a minimum of words. This time she surprised me completely.

'Bring her, do. She's reliable. Just don't get her killed too.'

I shook my head at her. 'You don't really believe this stuff about killing, do you?'

She stood there, swinging her spectacles on the chain. 'Yes, I believe it,' she answered finally. 'And I wish that I didn't. Be careful, my little Ross.' She kissed me on both cheeks, leaving behind strength and courage.

We went back to the drawing-room. Brown had covered three pages with his neat script. There was a detailed description of the photographs he had seen, a record of dates and amounts of heroin processed. He gave the pad to me diffidently.

'There are a few gaps but most of it's there. And it's accurate.'

I put the slips of paper at the back of my presscard. 'I'm on my way. I'll see you people when I get back. In the meantime whatever Ilinka says, do it.'

'And for a start, bed,' Ilinka said promptly. 'Phoebe can share my room. Mr Brown will go in the guest-room.'

We were still in the hallway when Phoebe was showing Brown the bathroom. I withdrew the bolts on the street-door.

'Whatever happens, I never felt so right in my life.

I'll be O.K., lovey. I know it.'

The square under lamplit snow was like an artist's impression of seventeenth-century Paris. One waited for the call of the night-watchman, the noise of sedan-chair bearers jogging over rock-hard pavement. I drove across the river and stopped outside the Ritz. A chasseur appeared from nowhere. I gave him the car-keys and told him to get the Renault off the street, that I'd collect it the following day. I carried my bag into the lobby. There's a timeless elegance about the Ritz that is beyond the dictate of fashion. Other hotels may match its luxury, none achieve its sophisticated charm. The good manners of the staff are a challenge to those of its guests. There were few people in the lobby and the travel-desk was closed. I left the bag with M. Potfer, made the long trek to the bar and asked if they could get me on a plane to London. There's little they can't do. I drank a whisky-sour while I waited and composed a letter. I wrote it on the hotel stationery.

> What you are looking for is for sale. I'll be in touch shortly. Macintyre.

I addressed the envelope to M. Paul Carnot at U.N.S.C.A.D headquarters, marking it Private and Personal. The barman told me that a first-class seat was available on the Air France flight leaving shortly after midnight. The ticket could be collected at Orly. I paid for my drink and walked back to the lobby. I mailed the letter and asked the switchboard to connect me with Baxter's office. The first edition would just about be going to press but he was on the line immediately.

'And about bloody time!' he bawled, telling someone

else to get off the wire. 'What sort of a game do you think you're playing? Didn't you get my cable? Why haven't you been in touch with Longman?'

'That's three questions,' I pointed out. 'Which do I answer first?'

His throat appeared to trouble him. 'Now look here, Macintyre, don't give me any of your double-talk. You're playing about with five hundred pounds of the newspaper's money. I demand to know what you're doing with it.'

The question wasn't unexpected. I'd no idea how Misty had managed to steer the idea past him in the first place.

'What are you doing with it?' His voice had become a tinny shout.

I glanced along the desk. M. Potfer was conducting an unseen and soundless orchestra, trilling and smiling as he totted up some figures on a piece of paper. The telephone cord was long enough for me to move away a couple of feet further. Baxter always sees a story in terms of banner headlines. That's the way I gave him this one.

'Stop,' he said hoarsely. I heard him draw a deep breath. 'Now look here, by George, Macintyre, have you completely gone off your head? I'm trying to get out a newspaper over here not a wrapper for fish-and-chips!'

I leaned an elbow on the counter, finding words that had been in my brain for months.

'If you'd like my contract instead I'll take the deal somewhere else. But I'll guarantee you'll make yourself the clown of the year. I'm offering you a twenty-four carat exclusive followed by a wrap-up feature with full pictorial coverage.'

Whatever else, Baxter's a pro. The balance tipped on

my side.

'Can you prove any of this stuff?' he asked cautiously.

'Everything that matters,' I said. 'I've got all the makings.'

It was his nose he cleared this time. 'I'm not so sure, Macintyre. By George. This newspaper has a reputation for accuracy.'

I was getting a little tired of his act. 'Like seventeen libel suits in a year, that's accuracy?' I challenged.

'How about *Paris-Match* and all those people? This is just the sort of thing they go for.'

'Not this one,' I said. 'They've all been warned off. *I've* been warned off. I'm telling you, these people are getting protection from the top. That's one of the reasons I've kept away from Longman. Crissakes, he'd be out there with a bloodhound and a magnifying-glass. You've got to let me have this one, Baxter. I want the whole magazine-section, colour-spreads, the lot.'

'You are definitely and positively insane,' he said. 'Come home at once.'

'I want that photographer who was with me in Rome,' I said. 'Jim Tully. What's he doing?'

I literally heard him swallow. 'He's around. I'm not sure.'

'Have him at the office nine o'clock tomorrow morning, ready to go to work in Paris. That reminds me, I'll need a passport.'

'Then go to Canada House,' he growled. 'What the hell happened to your old one anyway?'

'A passport in another name,' I explained patiently. 'Somebody else's passport. A forged passport if you like.'

His voice came from the narrow end of a funnel. 'Macintyre. Listen to me. Do you think this place is a supply-store for criminals?'

'Absolutely,' I said. 'I've seen you at work and I know where the bodies are buried. I don't care what name it is so long as the description is something like mine. They don't look that close.'

'They don't, huh?' Baxter mumbled something under his breath. 'I'm telling you I don't like this, Macintyre.'

'You like it,' I answered. 'As long as you're in the clear, you like it.'

His tone was suddenly stiff with formality. 'Are you listening to me, Macintyre? For the time being you're suspended. I don't even want you in the building. Do you hear me?'

'I hear you,' I answered. 'Don't forget Tully.'

He wasted a few seconds for prestige purposes. 'See Farrel about it,' he said at last.

'She'll be coming with me,' I said quickly and put the phone down. A written demand for my resignation would be in his desk just in case but my hunch was that I'd get what I'd asked for. My next call was to Misty. It was cold in London and she was still up watching television. Yes, she loved me.

'Put your woollies on,' I said. 'And get yourself out to Heathrow. You're meeting me there at five minutes after one. Air France.'

I paid for the calls, exchanged compliments with M. Potfer and rented the hotel limousine to take me out to Orly. The drive was a whisper of radials over the freezing hardtop, a constant flashing of yellow-beamed headlights. I switched on the reading-lamp and studied Brown's notes, scattering the torn pieces of paper along the auto-route. Bernanos had been putting out in the region of one hundred kilos of processed heroin every month. Considered the price in New York, delivered and uncut, the take became formidable, in the region of five million dollars a year. Brown's description of the Polaroid colour-prints was meticulous. Each feature a medium-built man in his fifties. The first photograph featured him at Longchamps, dressed in a seersucker suit and straw hat, consulting his race-card. The other two were street scenes. Brown noted that the guy might well limp. He based his feeling on the droop of a shoulder, the bend of a leg.

The limousine swung off the auto-route to where a complex of airport buildings dominated acres of parked cars, bus-bays and freight-hangars, the whole under concentration-camp lighting. My driver let me off in front of the Departure Hall. I walked through the electronic beam. There's a sense of theatre about Orly Airport at night, as if some Hollywood director has assembled a thousand extras. All are somewhat larger than life, caricatures of the roles they are playing. Plump African negresses swathed in vivid cotton prints, turbaned Sikhs, inscrutable Japanese. I recognised the Balkan spy in modish astrakhan, the bowler-hatted British diplomat, the Texan millionaire in his Italian silk suit. The police swarmed everywhere, distinguished by their hard-eyed stares whether plain-clothed or uniformed. I made my way towards the Air France desk feeling relaxed and sure of myself. There had to be a limit to these people's powers. They couldn't have the entire forces of law and order in their pocket. Key figures here and there, that's the way it would be. I could see it. Instructions would be passed laterally from one enforcement-agency to another and obeyed with no more question than any other order.

The girl at the desk had my ticket waiting. I took my bag across to the check-in point and put my bag on the scale. The attendant punched buttons on the panel in front of him. He handed me a red boarding-card offering the mechanical smile of those who work the night-shift.

'Gate sixteen, Monsieur. Your flight will be called in twenty minutes.'

It seemed a long way to the escalators. The customs officer sitting at the bottom ignored me completely. I showed my boardingcard and passport at the next desk. The cop flicked my passport open, checked the date of expiration and blocked a yawn delicately.

'Allez,' he waved. By French standards it was almost gracious.

I half-expected him to grab my hand as I retrieved my passport. But he didn't even notice when I looked back, halfway up the elevator. I'd seen the movies and I'd read the literature. This was ridiculous. Then it had to happen now, at the top of the steps. Chopper-faced men moving from behind pillars, closing in on me. All I could see was the usual throng of people round the Duty-Free shops. I bought a large bottle of scent for Misty, wondering how much longer we would last. I could see no way at all in which we could marry. A couple more years and she'd probably go the same way as the others, get smart and latch on to some nice guy who'd see that she puts her feet up when she's pregnant. A guy who'll talk to her about Sir Walter Scott, take her to the ballet and praise her spaghetti bolognese. She knows it and I know it but in the meantime we have as much going for us as most people, wedded or not – a respect and desire that is mutual.

I was still trying to pay for the scent when the flight was called. I bought a copy of Saturday's *Post* and hurried down the ramp. People were already boarding the big Boeing. A hostess collected my card and showed me into the first-class compartment. There was one other passenger, a smooth-haired man with spectacles sitting across the aisle. We nodded at one another. The next time I looked at him we were airborne and he'd clipped a pair of dark lenses over his spectacles. From the angle of his head he was dozing. I opened the newspaper and found the blurb for next Friday's Magazine-Section. There was an article by Jeff Canter, 'Scotland Yard Suspects New Protection Racket', a piece about the Lugano Film Festival and my own story on Lars Bjornsen, 'The Swedish Match Empire'. It had been written 'Emir'. I guessed Baxter's pencilling. There was literally no more time for a cigarette when the warning lights came on. A disembodied voice announced in two languages that we were beginning the descent to Heathrow. Would we fasten our seat-belts and extinguish our cigars and cigarettes. The weather in London was cloudy, the outside temperature seven degrees Centigrade. Our three-point landing was perfect. Invisible hands slowed our progress to a grumbling roll then we stopped. I yanked my bag from under the seat and was first off the plane.

A couple of hundred yards of corridor took me to the signs that send U.K. citizens one way, those from the Commonwealth and Aliens another. I'm in and out of Heathrow all the time and recognised the official who took my passport. He found a free space, rammed his stamp at the page and winked. There's something reassuring about landing in England after a trip abroad. The plain-clothes Immigration Officers, the Customs men dressed like naval officers, offer a suggestion of artlessness that conceals a highly-trained ability to detect fraud. I carried my bag through the Nothing To Declare exit. Misty was waiting just outside the doors, five feet-two of nothing dressed in a dark-blue trouser suit and black velvet cap. She'd had her hair cut since Thursday into a fringe and twin peaks that framed her cheeks. Winter never completely fades the freckles across the bridge of her nose and her mouth is usually on the brink of a smile.

We don't usually embrace in public but this was an exception, I took her arm and went down the escalator, past the grey-faced man touting for abortion-clinics and out to her M.G. It was as cold as in Paris and the lights were bright in the frosty air. Misty gave me the car-keys. The motor of her car is always as sweet as a berry. There's this racing-driver she knows who owns the garage where the M.G. is serviced. I switched on the headlights.

'What's all this about the press-attache?'

She was sitting like a boy, hands clasped round the knee that was on top.

'He phoned himself. The excuse was Michel Pelletier, the son-et-lumiere man.'

We were out of the tunnel and on the freeway. A strip of black hardtop unwound in the light of the lamps.

'How does Pelletier get in the act?'

She moved her head from side to side. 'There was some suggestion that you might like to do a profile of him but what this chap really wanted to know was what you were doing in Paris.'

'And did you tell him?' I asked.

'Yes. I told him you were doing a piece on Jean-Paul Texier but I don't think he was too convinced.'

It all tied up with what I'd been thinking earlier. Someone in the French Foreign Office would have called the Embassy in London and told them to run a check on me. There'd be no need to give a reason or if they did it would be a phony one. Everything these people did seemed to be done efficiently and intelligently. None the less, a chain's no stronger than its weakest link. I jerked my head back at the bag behind me.

'I brought you some scent.'

She puffed her mouth out. 'Scent, schment. Are you going to tell me what you're up to or not?'

'Positively,' I answered. 'I'm rescuing a clean-cut American boy from a fate worse than death, battling the evil forces of the Union Corse and giving myself an ulcer.'

'Are you in trouble?' she demanded.

I settled the low-slung sportscar at a steady sixty miles an hour.

'You might say that I'm working on it.'

Her frown offset her smile. 'I'll bet you one thing. Ilinka's mixed up in this somewhere.'

'Naturally,' I said.

She made a sound midway between impatience and anger. 'Does Baxter know?'

'I work for him, remember,' I said to pacify her. 'But I tell you *everything*.'

It took me the next quarter-hour. 'I've settled it with Baxter. You're coming back to Paris with me.'

Her first reaction was a squeal of delight. Her face sobered.

'Did you hear about Longman?'

'You tell me,' I suggested.

'Well,' she said. 'He sent me a telex message about a hundred yards long all about your lack of professional etiquette, common courtesy and so on. And it seems you burnt the top of his desk with a cigarette.'

'Tut,' I said. 'So what else is new?'

She screwed her head sideways, making a face at me. 'There are times when I'd like to pummel you, to beat you till you howl for mercy. You're so *bloody* conceited. Did you really mean that about me going back to Paris with you?'

I took a hand off the wheel and touched the softness of her thigh. 'I meant it. You're going to drive the getaway car with a spare rod tucked between your titties.'

Traffic-signals beyond the Hammersmith flyover blinked on cold empty streets. I drove the M.G. south into the sordid world of Earl's Court Road. The lights there were still bright, the coloured signs re-creating themselves over the steamed windows of the all-night restaurants. The entrance to the underground-station was crowded with butchy teenage girls, pot-peddlers and fags. Beyond it to the west were the lonesome expanses of bug-ridden rooming-houses, arrays of dirty milk-bottles and abandoned cars. I turned east on Fulham Road, along to the Forum Cinema then south down to Markham Street. It's a short thoroughfare with houses on each side, a trendy address for the young. The front doors are gaily-painted in primary colours and people grow shrubs in tubs. The incidence of burglary is high and nobody in his right mind over forty would care to live there. Misty's house has two bedrooms with a bathroom up on the second storey, a sitting-room and kitchen on the first. I put two wheels of the M.G. on the sidewalk like everyone else and killed the motor. Misty was already at her door. I lifted my bag from the back seat. A cat jumped from deep shadow and streaked across the playground opposite, ears flattened. Suddenly I felt very lonely.

'Are you coming in or not?' Misty demanded from her hallway.

We stood there looking at one another and I pushed the future out of my mind deliberately.

'There's no way of proving this,' I told her. 'At least no sure way. But when you go I'm going to be miserable.'

Her eyes searched mine briefly. 'What about me? Have you ever thought how I'll feel?'

'Often,' I said. 'And I'm never sure what the answer is.'

She rumpled my hair. 'Are you hungry?'

I shook my head. 'Just tired. A cup of coffee maybe.'

The small kitchen has yellow linen curtains and Design Centre furniture. The flower-and-bird tiles that line the top of the sink are souvenirs of our July vacation in Ibiza. There are plenty of souvenirs, memories that I hide from everyone except Ilinka. The syndrome has its ironies because while Misty dislikes Ilinka out of some basic jealousy, Ilinka's disapproval of our association is for an entirely different reason. She happens to think that I'm a born bachelor who's incapable of making any woman permanently happy.

The kitchen, the whole house, is always spotlessly clean. Misty does her own chores with the weekly help of a grim Finnish matron. She spooned coffee extract into a blue-striped cup, added boiling water and set the sugar-bowl in front of me. She sat down and leaned both elbows on the table.

'Why is it that a nice girl like me falls into the hands of a rake like you?'

The coffee was hot. I put the cup down again. 'Nobody in this day and age uses the word rake except for a garden implement.'

'A shit if you prefer the term,' she said composedly. 'A selfish, intolerant, egocentric shit.'

I unfastened my bag and put the bottle of scent on the table between us.

'You're forgetting the extravagance and untidiness. And I belch after eating stew and tend to be aggressive having drink taken. Open the package!'

In that, we're alike. Gifts have to be explored quickly. Her freckled nose shortened with pleasure and she rose to drop a mock-curtsy.

'Thank you, sir, kindly.'

The house is a gift from Misty's father, a Hampshire veterinary surgeon who holds that the indiscriminate use of insecticide has upset the ecological balance. He also collects butterflies. I've never met him but he appears to accept Misty's life-style without endorsing it. He's content that the rambling farmhouse on the outskirts of Andover will be there when she comes to her senses. In the meantime he knows that it's her own roof that's over her head. Some of the furniture belonged to her dead mother, the rest she brought herself. It's a house where two other people might easily have lived happily ever after.

I left the dirty mug where it was. A bachelor acquires a certain facility for ironing a shirt or washing a crock but the idea always offends Misty. She prepared a tray with biscuits and our morning tea. Neither of us normally bothers with breakfast.

'How about this Brown girl,' she asked very offhanded. 'What's she like?'

'A knock-out,' I said solemnly. 'Beautiful, intelligent and desperate. But I wouldn't trade your little finger for any or all of it. Boy Scout's honour!'

She was at the dresser with her back to me. 'Couldn't you do the rest from here, let someone else take over. The lawyer or Ilinka – she's supposed to know all the right people. Madame la Presidente Perpetuelle,' she added in a snotty voice.

'Turn around,' I said. 'Come on, *turn*!'

She did so, denying the tears that rolled down her face. I poked a finger at her like a pistol.

'I'm scared, kitten, but I can't let go. Nothing and nobody's going to stop me going back to Paris. It's like, maybe, the start of another life.'

She dashed the back of a hand at her cheek. 'What precisely is that supposed to mean?'

I gave her my handkerchief. 'I'll tell you when this is over.'

She blinked hard. 'I love you, Ross Macintyre.'

'That's nice,' I said and I believed her. I loved her too in my own odd way. 'I have a strong feeling that when the pressure is on the people at the top are going to walk away from this deal. And the fastest off the mark will be the big shots in the Union Corse. I don't care. What's left will be enough for us.'

She smiled at me shakily. 'I know it's going to be a wonderful story. Can we go to bed now, please?'

She went up first, leaving me to put the lights out downstairs. The white-carpeted bedroom was warm. She must have left the big heater burning all the time she'd been out. She was in the bathroom with the door shut. I started to undress, feeling as always the interloper in a world of romantic innocence. It was the two shelves of treasured Buchan and Dumas, the Constable prints of flat windswept landscapes, the disreputable teddybear chewed by generations of dogs. The bathroom opened and she stood there naked. Her skin was still faintly tanned and showing the marks of her bikini. She walked towards me, holding out her arms, her face framed in newly-brushed hair. The light went out and she was beside me. I found her lips with mine and tightened my grip. Desire set us alight and I took her hungrily. Her body arched to meet mine, her fingers twined in my hair. A great bird flew through my mind taking me with it beyond the far-away sky. Then I fell heavily, still locked in her arms and drifted into contentment. I loved her.

I must have slept soundly. The first thing I remember was a hand tugging my elbow. Misty was already dressed in her dark-blue trouser suit and wearing a pair of gold hoop-earrings I'd given her for her birthday. The small travelling clock on the table said a quarter after seven. She bent over the bed and ruffled my hair, the gesture an adieu to demonstrations of tenderness. It was another day and there was work to be done. The tea she had brought up was the way I like it, hot, sweet and strong. I looked at her over the rim of the mug.

'Did anyone ever tell you that you're a sight for sore eyes first thing in the morning?'

She inspected her nails, the tiny scissors ready to pounce. 'No-one except you, my love. I've packed my bag and run a bath for you. Don't come down till the milkman has gone.'

Her reasoning always seems to me to be wrong-way-round but that's Misty. She doesn't give a damn what the neighbours think but the milkman must never know that I'd slept at the house. By the time I was out of the bath, the bed was made and she was jockeying the hoover across the carpet. I carried our bags downstairs and poked my head round the kitchen door. The milk had been delivered.

'I'm going to make a quick run round the corner,' I said. 'I won't be more than a few minutes. Don't forget your passport.'

There are six apartments in my building. Mine is on the first floor, handy to the entrance. I opened my door to find a handful of slush mail strewn across the rug. An advertisement for an Escort Agency (twenty beautiful and aristocratic young ladies, some speaking two languages), a reminder that my driving-licence was due for renewal and an invitation to meet Abbie Hoffman. I threw the whole clutch in the waste basket. The flat smelled damp and cold. The rented furniture was cheerless in the grey morning light. Tenants in Wilberforce Court are mostly transient. I'd been there three years which made me the doyen of the building. A rhythmic bang-stretch-and-thud was coming from the apartment overhead. An Italian pizza manufacturer lives up there. He works out on a rowing-machine every morning. I changed into a pair of dark cord trousers, a blue cashmere shirt and topped them with the quilted car-coat Misty had given me. It was warm, light and left plenty of room for movement. *Plenty of room for movement?* This thing was going to my head. I kept trying to remember if my insurance policy covered mayhem. I transferred money and passport to my hip-pocket and called the answering-service. There were no messages. I let myself out of the apartment. The Italian's stroke-rate was up in the thirties.

Outside was the raw mixed smell of fog and bonfires that is London in November. Misty was sitting in the M.G. the motor running.

'Did you remember your passport?' I asked. She nodded and I gave her mine. If I was searched, I had to be clean.

I took the wheel and drove east through Sloane Square, skirting Buckingham Palace and into the Mall. Neither of us felt like talking. I joined the cortege of cars and buses that was snaking round Canada House into the Strand. The glass-concrete-and-aluminium building ahead was a monument to the founder of the *Post*. Parking-space on the lot at the back is allocated according to seniority. The names of the holders are stencilled into the hardtop. I backed the M.G. into my slot. Baxter's Rolls was in its own jumbo space, filthy dirty and showing what looked like a couple more dents in the fenders. Baxter keeps a bachelor flat in Albany but as often as not he sleeps up in the penthouse suite in the building. It was almost nine and people working the day shift were shoving through the entrances. I reached over and unfastened the door for Misty.

'You know what to do, sweetie. Make it as snappy as you can.'

I watched her small determined figure up the steps, through the doors with the *Post* emblem ground into the glass and across the lobby to the elevators. The starter gave her a salute and a smile and ushered her into the express. A familiar shape loomed behind Baxter's Rolls, inspected it with disdain and struck a match on the windshield. Jeff Canter is a tall man who wears elegant clothes and hats. He looked more like a successful actor than a crime-reporter. His pipe was belching smoke like a diesel-truck in low gear. He came across the parking-lot lifting his knees in a kind of hackney-action. I wound the window down.

'Hi, Jeff! Over here!'

He changed tack and fetched up, owl-eyed as he looked the car over. 'Where the hell have you just come from?' he demanded.

'Paris,' I said, opening the door for him to join me.

He just leaned against it, blowing the navy shag in my direction. His round unwinking eyes bore into me.

'They gave me your message. What is it you want?'

For my money Canter's the best crime-reporter in the business. His brother's an East End shyster and he'd been a cop himself but in spite of this people trust him. He gives his word reluctantly but once given he keeps it. The friendly advances were few when I first arrived from Canada. Most of them were from Canter. I fanned the fumes away.

'I need some electronic equipment,' I said, looking up at him. 'Is it all right for me to go see this man of yours?'

'Help yourself,' he said. His pipe had gone out. He struck another match, on the sole of his shoe this time and then forgot about it. 'Funny thing you wanting to see me. I was having a drink in this club last night and your name came up.'

I looked at him warily. Not only do we like one another, we're not even in competition. Anything he said would be free of snide intent.

'It could happen, I suppose,' I remarked.

Jeff has one of those mobile Jewish faces. Right now it

bore an expression of brooding suspicion.

'This was the Ark Club in Soho. I go there five nights a week. The pimp who runs it passes on the odd piece of information. It was the man with him who asked about you, a Frenchman. If I worked on the *Post* then I'd know you, he said. He read your articles etcetera. I asked him which ones but he couldn't remember.'

I would have given a lot to be able to level with him and ask his advice but I didn't have the right. I shook my head.

'That's not really my scene, a pimp. I haven't as much as had a drink with a whore in over eighteen years.'

Canter rested his chin on the top of the window, his Dunhill pipe still mercifully extinct.

'You're missing the point, buster. The Frenchman was no pimp. He just chose to act like one. I checked. His name's Tomaso Azzopardi and he's a Corsican wine-importer.'

I did my best to run the bluff past him. 'Probably a genuine lover of style. What's Nagle's exact address?'

'Two hundred and forty Wilton Street, behind Victoria Station.' He sniffed. 'You're sure there's nothing you want to tell me?'

'Like what?' I parried.

He turned the sniff into a chuckle. 'Get stuffed!'

He strutted across the parking-lot into the building. If Union Corse agents were making inquiries about me in London it would be because they expected me to stay there. The clock on top of the building said twenty after nine. The half-hour struck before Misty hurried out and across to the car. She plopped herself down, put a plain brown envelope in my lap and spoke in a tight voice.

'You'll never get away with it.'

I tore the envelope open. Inside was a British passport made out in the name of John Pettifer, born 1936, occupation clerk. His hair was brown, his eyes blue. The photograph on the opposite page showed a man whose hair was roughly the same length as mine and wearing spectacles.

'You'll never get away with it,' Misty repeated.

I put the blue folder in an inside pocket, Memorising the details. Born Colchester, Essex, 14th November, 1936.

'A pair of spectacles and peak-hour traffic. What do you want to bet?'

She wriggled with exasperation. 'Oh, what's the good! The envelope was on my desk. Baxter telephoned to say that when Pettifer leaves the building tonight he's going to report the loss of his passport.'

'And the best of British luck to him,' I said. 'The interview between him and Baxter may have been something. Where does this guy work?'

'Accountancy. I got the tickets.' She produced them, one in her name the other in the name of Pettifer. 'Tully took his. I told him that we're all supposed to be strangers at the airport. That he's to go straight to his hotel and wait till you get in touch. He's got a room at the Claridge.'

It's a small hotel on Champs-Elysees and popular with Americans. It was close to Susini's office and the staff would be used to seeing tall men carrying cameras.

'And where are you staying?' I demanded.

She glanced sideways, lifting her chin. 'The Balmoral. It's on the Left Bank.'

'I know where it is,' I told her. 'Five hundred yards from Ilinka's place. What are you trying to prove?'

She ignored the question to use her lipstick. 'I hope you'll remember what I said when I'm visiting you in prison.'

I cocked my head. 'And what was that?'

Her voice was disgusted. 'Ah, why should I care. It's your life. If you don't need the car I'd better leave it in the garage.'

I took my bag from the seat. 'I'll take a cab. If anything should happen at Heathrow – I mean with the police – call Ilinka immediately.' I slid out of the seat and she took the wheel, sticking out her tongue at me. I had a feeling that none of us really knew what we were getting into with the possible exception of Ilinka. I'd started off as Cool Hand Luke but that seemed a long time ago. I walked west to the Strand and found an incurious oculist who fixed me up with a pair of plain-lensed spectacles. The heavy frames were similar to the ones Pettifer was wearing in the passport photograph. A cab took me as far as the Victoria end of Vauxhall Bridge Road. I made my way down mean streets, past cut-price stores, dusty windows filled with trash from three continents, Japanese sword-sticks and nylon anoraks. Peddlers were selling fruit in the gutters, stamping beside the glowing coke-braziers. There was a sense of bawdy good nature about the neighbourhood. Boards advertised the personal services of beautiful Swedish models, exotic young coloured actresses and so on. A neon sign above a store ran endlessly, composing the words.

*N*A*G*L*E*S*E*L*E*C*T*R*O*N*I*C*S*

Black paper gummed over the inside of the display window prevented passers-by from seeing in. I pushed the door and a buzzer sounded in the back. A quantity of hifi and stereo equipment, radios and television sets of all kinds, were arranged haphazardly under overhead strip-lights. The articles were connected by lengths of steel chain.

'Anyone in?' I called.

'If the door's open somebody's in. Always.' The voice came from a fattish man standing by a card that proclaimed NAGLES KNOWLEDGE COSTS MORE: THE BEST ALWAYS DOES.

He was a fattish man in a dirty dustcoat whose head was too large for his neck. His grey hair sprung rather than grew and his nose and mouth were askew, as if some sculptor with an eye on the clock had added them at random. Beyond him was a small office where a large girlie calendar hung behind a desk. The desk, chairs and carpet belonged in a junkyard.

I'd been hearing about Nagle ever since I arrived in England. The first time was when a bunch of guys hit on that Bond Street bank using electronic equipment to run the clock on a time-vault forward and empty the place of three-quarters of a million pounds. Old-timers in the bars along Fleet Street wagged their heads and said 'Jungle-face Jake'. Industrial spying, the divorce trade, the top operatives were supposed to get their apparatus from Nagle. Scotland Yard left him severely alone and Canter always claimed this was because they used him themselves. Whichever way you looked at it, in his own field Nagle was the final authority in the country. He was also a character, closing the store three afternoons a week and going to the track where he was known as one of the big cash gamblers.

'Jeff Canter sent me,' I volunteered.

'Did he, the schmuck! With tipsters like him who needs the tax collectors? You got a friend who's a jockey as well, Charley?'

'I couldn't afford it,' I answered and followed him into the office. The chair he offered was covered with diagrams done in Chinese ink. He put a kettle on a gas-ring on the floor. There was a teapot and cups on the dirty unswept carpet, a carton of milk and a sack of sugar. He eyed me slyly and padded out to lock the street-door, his feet in holed tennis-shoes. He came back, rubbing his misshapen nose.

'What do you do for a living, then, Charley?'

I'd heard that his manner was strange and I wasn't buying his charm.

'I'm in the same line as Canter,' I said.

The flimsy kettle shifted under the heat of the flame. 'I like to know who I'm doing business with,' he said, revealing a mouthful of unconvincing teeth. 'At least when it's a special job. You're not looking for no Solid State Special Six transistor, are you?'

The room was stuffy and stank of battery acid. I loosened my coat.

'Not exactly, no. It's not too easy to explain.'

'Try me,' he said, leaning forward.

I took my time lighting a cigarette. 'I'm going into a house to have a discussion with someone. I told you, I'm a reporter. I want this talk to be recorded. The man I'm interviewing will know this. That's the problem.'

He cocked his head, pouring water into the teapot. 'Are you a poker-player, Charley?'

'I gave it up,' I said. 'Incidentally, the guy I'm going to see will know all about your gadgets.'

'Bollix,' he answered sharply. 'The only one who

knows all about my gadgets is me.'

He shoved a cup of tea across the table. The inside of the cup was stained with tannin. I took a sip. I'd tasted worse. Nagle was gulping his, making a noise like a high-blowing thoroughbred. I reached for the ash-tray.

'What I mean is that he's of a scientific turn of mind.'

'Nice,' he approved. '"Scientific turn of mind." So enough, already and let me think.' He covered his nose with the palm of his hand, letting his eyes roam freely. I waited until he was ready to share his deliberations, pondering the girl on the calendar.

He snapped his thumb and forefinger. 'I've got it, Charley. It *is* Charley, isn't it?'

I shrugged. 'You like it, why not?'

'Good, old boy,' he said. 'Good old boy, Charley. What type residence is the place you're referring to?'

'It's an area something like Hampton Court, Richmond, somewhere like that. Houses with gardens, avenues with trees, that sort of thing.'

He spooned the moist sugar from the bottom of his cup into his mouth with relish.

'I'm thinking about a unit that'll give you quality reproduction at ranges up to a mile. Would that be enough?'

'It sounds O.K.,' I said.

'How much you want to spend?' he said looking down his nose. 'One, two, three, five?'

'Hundred?'

His expression changed. 'The last of the big-time spenders and Canter sends him to me! Look, Charley, you got a problem and that costs.'

'The one thing I haven't got is time,' I said pointedly.

He locked all the drawers in his desk and hauled himself up. He opened another door and switched on lights. The windows of the warehouse were covered with steel shutters. Cases stencilled in English, German and Japanese were stacked round the walls. Nagle moved among them with the certainty of a terrier tracking a rat. Suddenly he stopped and slit open an oblong package with a jack-knife. Under the wrappings was a beautifully-grained black leather dispatch-case. Nagle sprang the locks. The interior looked conventional. There were places for documents, stationery and the like. He lifted out a false bottom, revealing a network of wires soldered to a copper sheath. He dropped the bottom back, closed the case and flourished his cuffs and wrists like a conjuror at a childrens' party. He turned the handle of the case over on the other side.

'One, two, three,' he intoned. He opened the dispatch-case again. His recorded voice came back at us from a hidden speaker.

I shifted my weight from the packing-case where I'd been leaning.

'That's very impressive but then there's a lot of people beside us who must have seen the movie.'

He put his thumb on the well-tooled leather. 'You're not with me, Charley. This is your bait. Only the mugs buy these things. That's what you want your man to take you for, isn't it? A first-class unpruned and purely simple mug?'

He answered his own question. 'Of course you do. So the geezer finds this gear and he's satisfied. He doesn't know what we know. I'm going to show you a real professional job, Japanese, of course. You ever hear of a Japanese Jew, Charley?'

I was running out of time and temper rapidly. 'Not

by name, no.'

He shook his head. 'I never heard of one, neither though it stands to reason there's got to *be* some.'

My voice was a little unsteady by now. 'Are you going to sell me this stuff or not.'

He rolled his head at me. 'I keep getting these vibes about you, Charley. I think you're a bit of a desperado.'

He turned round, presenting a broad butt as he rooted among the packing-cases. My foot itched to plant him squarely in the middle of them. He straightened up, breaking the seals on a narrow box. The leather belt he produced was made of ordinary cowhide with a round metal clip-in buckle like those on scout-belts. Next out of the box was a battery-operated razor. He gave it to me to hold, draped the belt round his dustcoat and waddled into the office. His voice took me by surprise, emerging from the razor in my hand. He appeared again, wearing his lopsided smile, Jungle-face Jake the Children's Entertainer.

'You see, Charley,' he said. 'This ain't something out of a novelty store. This is your actual gear and it works. They only made fifty of them and I took the only ten in Europe. Everything you need in a belt and a razor. Two hundred and fifty quid that and the dispatch-case, less five for cash, two hundred and forty.'

I took the clip of bills from my hip-pocket. 'Your arithmetic's lousy.'

He held his hand out. 'But I'm a nice feller when you get to know me.'

He carried the electronic apparatus into the office and wiped every inch of it with a duster, occasionally holding the pieces up to the light. He waved.

'There you go, mate. It's all yours. Take it away.'

I packed the razor and belt inside the dispatch-case. With my travelling bag I now had a double handful. I looked at him and grinned.

'Thanks for everything, Charley.'

He had style, I'll admit it. 'My pleasure,' he replied. 'Keep your batteries nice and sharp and leave the door open when you go out.'

Victoria Station was a block away. I carried the two bags into the vast glass-dome building. Noises echoed sombrely, the hollow-voiced public-address announcements, the grind of metal on metal, the klaxons of the electric baggage-carriers. The faces in the crowds reflected a sullen acceptance of discomfort, of strikes and power-cuts, of indifferent or fearful management. It was moments like this that prompted me to look for my island. The labour-force was eighty per cent coloured and primed by the Race Relations Act to kick John Bull's ass whenever they felt like it. Even the station bums were a poorer breed. Gone were the self-styled majors who would sidle up with a pitch about a misplaced wallet, the confused elderly bodies looking for a long-lost sister through a haze of gin. Their successors were tangle-haired drop-outs who sprawled on the benches, fingering their needle-sores. When the man said move, they moved, without protest or even token defiance.

I called the United States Consulate from a booth in the ticket-hall. A woman with a New England accent dealt with my inquiry. Yes, indeed, F.I.D.A., Federal Investigation of Drug Addiction, an agency independent of the United States Bureau of Narcotics and controlled from the White House itself, maintained offices in Europe, in Paris and Rome to be precise. The address of the Paris office, one moment, please. It was 14 bis, Rue

D'Aguesseau, right behind the American Embassy. She spelled bis for me twice and I hung up. I took the underground to Gloucester Road, and walked the short distance from there to the West London Air Terminal.

There was no sign of Misty or Tully so I boarded a bus and took a seat upstairs. A couple of minutes later we were on our way to Heathrow. The hint of fog was still strong. Lamps burned dimly in the stores and down a hundred identical streets. Where television masts spiked the roofs and frozen wet-wash hung in grimy backyards. Once we'd passed Chiswick and were on the overhead motorway, the scene changed. The office-buildings and factories were ablaze with light, their top floors paralleling the passing traffic. Shirtsleeved men worked in sub-tropical temperatures behind glass like trained chimpanzees. Come five o'clock, they'd be heading back for the television-masts, the sausage-and-mash suppers, the renewed bickering with the woman who only yesterday had been a lover. Yet it was the diet that kept most people happy. Deep down I acknowledged the fact that Ilinka was right – there were too many hills for me to climb, too many mazes to explore. Sure, a woman might accept it as a life-style but in the end it would destroy her.

We were nearing the cut-off that leads to the airport. People round me were getting their things together, their faces as dull as their conversation had been. I was quickly into the Departure Hall, carrying my two bags. Flight-time was in twelve minutes. I climbed the steps to the bar, bought myself a cold beer and took it through to the cafeteria area. I was well placed to see customs and immigration officials below. Jim Tully was leaning against the wall, blond and reticent, sucking on a match. He was dressed in a trenchcoat with a fox-fur collar and his owl-eye camera was slung round his neck. I'd worked with him a couple of years before in Rome. We'd been trying to get a story together on one Emilio Venturi, the scandal-hound, first and greatest of the post-war paparazzi. It turned out that for once we had an unwilling subject, a scooter-borne ghost with an evil smile and a whole raft of ideas about fighting a rear-guard action. We chased him into Trastevere avoiding the bottles thrown by his chums as we proffered bundles of lire. We'd finally given up and Tully and I had spent the rest of the night together. He was Australian, I was Canadian, and we worked on the same newspaper. The conversation, the sober part of it, anyway, fascinated me. Tully had built his own camera, using what he called the 'principle of image-intensification'. I learned that there is no such thing any more as the cover of darkness. Tully proved it by putting a rock through a street-lamp and taking a picture of me at twenty yards using no more light than the cigarette burning in my mouth. The print came out as clear as day. People have offered him a lot of money for his invention, research facilities, but Tully doesn't budge easily.

The hands of the clock notched off another six minutes and one of those cool snooty English voices sounded throughout the building.

'Will Mr Pettifer, passenger to Paris on Air France dah-dah-dah please come to the dah-dah-dah immediately. This is the last call for Mr Pettifer, passenger to Paris on the dah-dah-dah.'

It was my cue. Tully eased himself off the wall and drifted away with the stragglers. I ran down the steps, waving my ticket frantically. A girl in uniform wasted no time. My bags were weighed and a boarding-card stuck in my hand. The girl hurried me towards the waiting officials. I placed Pettifer's passport on the desk, my stomach turning over. I'd no idea what my face was registering but the picture in my mind was clear enough. I saw a detention-room, a ring of cops watching as I emptied my pockets. I pushed the spectacles up on my nose as the immigration-officer glanced at me. The girl saved me, wiggling her butt between us, her voice anxious.

'He's supposed to be on the 420 and we've got less than three minutes to make it.'

He rolled a bawdy eye. 'I'd want a lot longer than that with you, darling.' Then miraculously the passport was in my unsteady hand. The two bags had been checked through to Orly. We sprinted down the corridors, the girl's movements hampered by her tight skirt. The jet motors were roaring when we reached the plane. A steward hauled me aboard and slammed the hatch shut. I dropped into the one vacant seat at the back and fastened the straps. When I opened my eyes again I was airborne and travelling on another man's passport. It was as simple as that. I shook my head at the offer of a newspaper. Misty stood up six rows ahead, her eyes anxious till she had found me. Tully's blond head was near the front.

The suspense had gone and I felt somehow cheated. The feeling of let-down had something to do with being on the plane. Land boundaries have a dramatic value that is unique. You see these two frontier-posts, the bridge or stretch of no-man's-land, and you realise that the distance between them can be the difference between life and death. The sense of urgency is somehow lost on a boat or plane. The hostesses were handing round landing-cards that had to be completed for the police on arrival. Name, nationality, number of passport and port of entry. I signed the card with a fair imitation of the signature on Pettifer's passport. I kept telling myself that a document that was good enough for the British would satisfy the French. If the logic was faulty I didn't want to hear about it.

My seat was next to the aisle. An elderly American couple next to me pressed the buzzer and asked for iced water. I stood to give the hostess room, glancing forward automatically. The curtain dividing the first-class compartment from tourist was only half-drawn. Sitting beyond it was the Frenchman who had been on the plane with me earlier that day. I retreated behind a map of Europe, making no sense of it. Optimism tried to make out a case. There were probably hundreds of businessmen who did the round-trip between Paris and London every day. The man had sat next to me for almost an hour without giving me a second look. I forced myself to read until the cabin darkened suddenly. The plane dropped out of sunshine and pierced the cloud ceiling. The geometrical strips of highway criss-crossed fields far below, piebald where the snow had melted. Orly sucked us into the last banked spiral and run-in. The pilot taxied the plane to the arrival-bay. There was the usual scramble for hats and coats. I moved along the line, neither at the front nor at the back. My spectacles were in place and I was holding my passport with the landing-card tucked inside. As far as hope would take me, I *was* John Pettifer. The conviction started to fade as we shuffled towards the blue uniforms waiting at the desks. I'd read that there are five hundred thousand people deemed to be undesirable visitors to France. I'd read about the computer banks, the spot-checks made on incoming passengers. I found myself fervently hoping that Pettifer had never disgraced himself here.

The cop I drew was a Negro with a Ronald Colman moustache. He reached for the passport, flicking the landing-card aside with a practised gesture. Expressionless eyes held me for what seemed to be an eternity then he motioned me on through the barrier. I walked as fast as I dared, collected my bags and took them through customs. I was halfway across the vast hall when a girl's voice came over the public-address system.

'Will M. Pettifaire, passengaire from London to Paris, please come to the Information Desk. M. Pettifaire, please.'

I'm fairly certain that my step didn't falter though an entire alarm system was ringing in my head. No-one in Paris was supposed to know my name and there could be no convincing reason why the airline would want me. I put my bags down at the post office guichet and went through the motions of writing out a telegram. I could see the Frenchman from the first-class compartment crossing the hall. He moved his head slightly as he passed the Information Desk. I knew the gesture had registered with the couple standing there talking to the Air France employee. Tully vanished into a cab. Misty was fifty yards away, floating round the flower-shop, agitatedly. The couple at the Information Desk had a map spread out between them. The man's interest was clearly somewhere else. His head swung like a snake's as he talked, scanning anyone who chanced to come near. I stepped into a phone-booth and dialled Ilinka's number.

'I'm at Orly. I've come through customs and immigration but there's something very strange going on.' I told her what.

Her voice was as clear as if she were standing beside me. 'Leave the airport immediately. Your call from the Ritz was monitored at the Centrale.'

I put the phone down as if it were radio-active and walked away keeping my back to the Information Desk. Misty followed me out to the bus and took the seat beside me. She spoke very quietly.

'I'm scared.'

I sneaked a look at our neighbours. 'They monitored my call to Baxter. They must have known I was coming back.'

Her face was shocked. 'How could they do that?'

I snapped my lighter for her. 'Easy. Those cops took the number from the list at the hotel. All they needed was someone on their side at Centrale. They've got people everywhere. Why not there?'

The big bus swung out on to the auto-route. I felt her hand creep into my pocket.

'Why didn't they stop you at the airport, the police or someone?'

I was trying to work it out myself. 'Because they must have changed their minds. It has to be the note I wrote to Carnot. He'd have gotten it first thing this morning. They decided they wanted me back in France.'

Her hand tightened in mine. 'It's all too ridiculous,' she said stoutly. 'I refuse to believe you can't just stop this bus and call the nearest policeman. This isn't the Congo for God's sake!'

Misty's faith in the established order is supreme. I tried to explain, keeping my voice down to baffle the guy behind who was leaning forward. It could have been Misty he was interested in but I was taking no chances.

'These people have hitch-hiked into every law-enforcement agency in the country. Accept that and the blinkers are off.'

She shook her head. 'I can't believe it. Life isn't like that.'

'*Yours* isn't,' I corrected. 'Give me my own passport back. If I'm going to be buried it might as well be in my right name.'

She turned away, uptight and furious. 'You make me sick, Ross. You're actually enjoying all this deep down. Being the centre of attraction, having people worry about you.'

She was right but only in a limited way. What was happening now was a defiance of conformity, a rejection of a safe job, slippers by the fire, all the things Misty wanted for me. I opened her purse and exchanged Pettifer's passport for my own.

'Send this off to Baxter as soon as you've checked in, registered mail and don't move from the hotel till you hear from me.'

She shook her head, blinking back the tears. Her voice was barely loud enough to hear.

'You needn't think I don't know.'

I half-turned, sending the guy behind back on his seat. Then I put my arm round her shoulders.

'What is it that you know, baby?'

Her smile was resigned. 'That I can't change you.'

'But you'd like to,' I insisted.

'Not even that,' she said steadily. 'You give me what you can and it's always been enough.'

I put my mouth against her ear. 'I'm getting off here. Keep your eyes open for anything unusual. I'll call you in a couple of hours' time.'

I walked up the aisle and asked the driver to let me off. He unlocked the baggage-hatch, hanging in there like a hawk till I gave him a couple of coins. I watched the bus out of sight. No-one else had left it. No cars had stopped nearby. Nevertheless, I changed cars twice on the way to the Ritz. M. Potfer produced Ilinka's car-keys and I dropped the spectacles in a nearby waste basket. The multi-storey garage was three blocks away. They had put the Renault on one of the upper floors. A sign in the waiting-room gave me an idea, cars for rent with or without driver. I tapped the glass dividing the waiting-room from the office area. A girl slid the partition back.

'Tell them to leave my car where it is,' I said. 'I need something bigger for a few days.'

She rang a bell. A mechanic showed me a black Peugeot 404 with fuel injection. It was similar to a hundred others in the city. I produced my driver's licence, filled in a couple of forms and paid a deposit. There was a good feeling about the sturdy vehicle, a suggestion that it would still keep going minus a side and two wheels. I stowed my bags in the trunk and drove out on to Place de la Madeleine. The hiring made sense. Carnot's people might well have access to the files in the licencing-bureau. If they ever saw me driving Ilinka's car, a check on the plates would lead them straight to Place des Religieuses. It was almost one o'clock and I had to eat. I bought myself a steak and cheese in a gaslit bar staffed by waiters wearing handle-bar moustaches and striped aprons. The place was patronised by chorus-boys from the Lido and no self-respecting hood would have been found dead in it.

I had no idea how many people were out looking for me or whether the police were actively involved. I was certain of one thing, however. The man directing operations against me would not be thrown by one small setback. He would know by the monitored call that I was coming back to Paris and how. What I hoped was that he would accept my new role as the venal journalist, the reporter turned extortioner. The production at Orly had been casual to the point of sloppiness. Someone must have picked up the phone, called the Information Desk and left some sort of fake message for me. The couple there wanted to have a good look at me. The hunt appeared to be divided into three groups, those who knew me by name, either Macintyre or Pettifer. Those who simply had my description and the few who knew me by sight. The one question I couldn't answer was how they knew the name I was travelling under. Nobody had handled Pettifer's passport except Baxter, Misty and me. And the Negro cop at Orly. The way things were going, the afterthought wasn't outrageous.

I finished the last of my coffee and paid the check. It was ten minutes to two. I walked back to where I'd left the Peugeot in a paid-parking lot. The cloud ceiling had lowered, darkening the city. I drove north, circled the Arc de Triomphe and anchored the car in front of Susini's building. I was betting on him being a quick luncher. Ten minutes went by and he appeared, coming from the direction of Avenue Kleber. He was hatless, dressed in what looked like a vicuna overcoat and leading a brindled bulldog on a leash. I beeped the horn softly and wound down the window as he neared the car. He came to a halt, the bulldog sinking down on the pavement, stump-tail twitching.

Susini showed all his teeth. 'M. Macintyre! That is really a coincidence. I was just thinking about you.'

I nodded. 'I'm glad I caught you. I didn't really want to go into the office. I have my reasons.'

He leaned against the side of the car his expression solicitous. 'Can I be of any help?'

I pulled my eyes away from the driving-mirror. 'I don't think I'm being followed, not at the moment at any rate. But there's a good chance that I will be.'

His voice was quite casual. 'I'd say that was certain. And I wouldn't return to Gunn's Hotel if I were you.'

I blinked. 'Thanks for the tip. If there's more you'd better get in the car.'

He reached over the top of the window and unfastened the door. The bulldog went over the front seat and settled in the back. Susini stretched his long legs, smiling faintly.

'You can count yourself lucky that I am not a member of the Union Corse.'

'Why don't we skip the fencing?' I asked. 'I'm too ham-fisted for the rapier.'

He wriggled an elegant shoulder. 'You mustn't be annoyed with me, M. Macintyre. It is all much simpler than it appears. I know someone who works at the *Controle des Etrangers*. In my profession one is obliged to make use of such people. Your story intrigued me yesterday. I learned that a M. Ross Macintyre had been registered at Gunn's Hotel, Place des Vosges. It turned out that the hotel belonged to yet another Canadian.'

A police-car flashed by, made the full circle and took a second look at the Peugeot. Susini lifted a hand and the police-car took off.

'Yeah, well,' I said. 'I hope you do as well for me when the time comes.'

'Better.' His gold bridgework glinted. 'I can guarantee that. My motives happen to be as self-centred as yours.'

'Shall we finish waltzing?' I suggested.

He offered me his cigarette-case, gold with a slide-action. 'I understand you to be a journalist representing a powerful newspaper. That might make you careless. The truth is that you are in serious danger at this moment. Do I make myself clear?'

'Crystal,' I answered.

His eyelids were hoods of flesh-coloured satin that hid his thoughts for a second.

'In fact your life is safe only as long as the Browns are safe. But I don't suppose any of this is news to you?'

'None of it,' I agreed. 'Suppose we talk about these motives of yours.'

He pushed his chin forward, touching the deep cleft with a fore-finger.

'They are political, Monsieur. I am an ambitious man.'

I could accept that. Ambitious and highly intelligent. 'One question,' I said. 'Do you think you know where the Browns are?'

'Good God, no,' he said quickly. He looked genuinely shocked. 'Let me explain, M. Macintyre. You said enough yesterday to give me the lead I needed. We are used to solving riddles in my office. I have an assistant with an imaginative turn of mind. The papers on the Brown case were delivered to me at two o'clock this morning.'

The bulldog was snuffling noisily on the back seat. Susini stretched behind and quietened the animal.

'I'm waiting for the proposition,' I said.

His overcoat *was* vicuna, his shoes made of crocodile-skin. But the coat was dark-blue and the shoes were dyed black. There was nothing flashy about his appearance or manner. He turned his palm over.

'Once I had the key-piece, the others fell into place. An hotel frequented by the Brotherhood. An U.N.S.C.A.D. chemist in jail on a trumped-up rape charge, another was dead. And all these elements linked together by a reporter of some repute. What else *could* it mean but drugs, heroin to be precise?'

I raised my head. 'There's one thing I'm not quite clear about. Suppose I hadn't come here this afternoon?'

He almost smiled, content that the thought reached his eyes. 'You had to come here. You need me. I even left word where I would be lunching.'

I watched the traffic for a few seconds, trying to make up my mind how far I could trust him. I decided to gamble, to tell him a little more than he already knew but not as much as he'd wish.

'I left Paris at midnight,' I said. 'Warned off by the police. I used a false passport to return.'

He held his hand out. 'Let me have it. I'll take care of it for you. We want no unnecessary complications.'

'It's on its way back where it came from,' I answered. 'My own is in my pocket. I'm prepared to swear that I used it to enter France again.'

He made a tent with his hands, peering into it as he talked. 'I know a judge, a man of immense influence in legal circles. He and I happen to think alike politically. Your story would be of great interest to him. If we could prove it, I could guarantee complete exoneration for Brown and his sister.'

'I'll have the proof before the night is out,' I said, looking at him.

His face was serious. 'You're not a fool, M. Macintyre. No matter what cards you have, remember who you are playing with. That number I gave you will reach me at any hour of the night or day. As soon as you're ready, call me.'

He unfastened the door. The bulldog hurdled the seat and lifted a leg against the front wheel. Susini smiled.

'A sign of good-luck. A bientot, M. Macintyre.'

I drove down Champs-Elysees, made the turn on Place de la Concorde and stopped under the bone-bare trees on the edge of the gardens. The walks were deserted, the carrousels boarded-up. The area is a sensitive one for the police. There's the Elysee-Palace, official residence of the Presidents of France, the British Embassy behind it, next to the United States Embassy. The neighbourhood is a focal point for demonstrators in times of political crises. The barriers are never far away and the police are always in evidence. I could see them now, scattered in pairs along the embassy walls, lurking in the driveways.

The house I wanted was a narrow-fronted affair, squeezed in between a post office and an annexe to the Ministry of the Interior. The long thin windows were well-curtained and impossible to see through. A modest plaque on the street-door said:

FEDERAL INVESTIGATION OF DRUG ADDICTION

There were two unmarked bell-pushes. I pressed both of them. The door opened very suddenly. If I'd been leaning against it, I'd have fallen flat on my face.

The man standing in the hallway was wearing a dark suit, a button-down collar and wing-tipped black shoes.

He was solidly built with the sort of face you sometimes see on a Boston cop. A little pugnacious, steady blue eyes, a big chin and hair the colour of pine sawdust. He stuck the word between us like a buffer.

'Yes?'

The floor of the panelled hallway was carpeted. I could see some straight-backed chairs and a pendulum clock. I produced my presscard. He eyed it briefly and shook his head.

'Not a chance, Buddy. You want to state your requirements in writing.'

He was wearing a tie-clip with some sort of insignia. I've had a fair amount of experience with U.S. Government officials in Europe. They've issued me passes to enter their military zones. I've hung around consulates, waiting to have documents notarised. I've noted a certain reluctance to perform their function – as if they were department-store Santas scared of running out of gifts.

'I'm here on your business,' I said steadily. 'And you're going to have to throw me down these steps to get rid of me!'

He spread his legs a little wider as an older man appeared from the back of the hallway, a man in his mid-sixties with silver hair and rimless spectacles. He was wearing a blue suit and a polka-dotted bow-tie that matched his pocket-handkerchief. He looked like a banker or a high-class con-man. He beckoned me inside and told his companion to shut the street-door. We stood for a moment, the smell of beeswax strong, the clock ticking away. Then the older man gave a little bow.

'Would you care to come in here, sir. You too, Glen.'

The large room overlooked the street. There were

two sets of curtains, more panelling, bookshelves and metal filing-cabinets. A small United States flag rose out of an untidy heap of papers on the desk.

The older man seated himself in a swivel-chair. 'May I have your name, sir?' he asked courteously. He made a note of it on the pad in front of him. There was a large safe at his side, the kind of thing you usually see in a jeweller's office.

'I'm Harold Spitz. This is my colleague, Glen Duryea. What can we do for you, Mr Macintyre?'

'I'm going to tell you a story about heroin,' I said. I was edgy but I tried not to show it. 'It'll take some time.'

Spitz considered the ceiling overhead, his chubby cheeks serene. Duryea was smiling like a kid who's been told to watch his manners.

'Get the machine, Glen,' said Spitz.

Duryea opened a deep closet in the panelling and wheeled out a trolley carrying a professional-size tape-deck. He touched a button. A light glowed. His nail tapped the mike sending a hollow sound echoing round the room. He sat down again.

'Regulations.' Spitz had a trick of following his speeches with a little movement of the head, a kind of implicit assurance that what he said was correct.

These people weren't essential to me but having them on my side would be a definite advantage. I smiled.

'Maybe I'll get a copy of the tape.'

Their own smiles came and went quickly as if I'd just told a tale that was in dubious taste. I watched the revolving tapes for a while then cleared my throat.

'Ross Macintyre, Canadian citizen, speaking in the Paris office of the United States Bureau of Narcotics and Dangerous Drugs. The date, November, nineteen-seventy-two, the time approximately fourteen hours twenty. How am I doing, gentlemen?'

It was provocative, childish even, but they were setting the pace.

'Pretty good,' said Spitz. 'You've obviously had experience.'

I told the story as it stood, starting with the death of Bernanos in Fontainebleau Forest. The only thing I didn't reveal was where the Browns were hiding. Spitz brought his fingertips together.

'This office is grateful for your co-operation, Mr Macintyre. We'll see that this information is passed on to the appropriate local authority.'

It was a second or so before his meaning sank in. '*The appropriate local authority!*' I spluttered.

Spitz wagged his head at me encouragingly. His accent was that of a first-year French student.

'*L'Office Centrale de Repressions du traffic illicite de stupefiants.* We ourselves have no standing here in law, Mr Macintyre.'

'Hold it,' I said, sticking my hand in the air. 'You people know far more about the Union Corse than I ever will. They're killers and they've infiltrated every law-enforcement agency in the country.'

Both faces stared back impassively. I tried again, beginning to sound desperate.

'Why do you suppose that this Office Centrale etcetera hasn't clobbered any of these bastards. I'll *tell* you why. They're probably up to their necks in the caper themselves!'

It was no good. I read it in Spitz's eyes, the way he spread his hands.

'I'm sorry. I appreciate your position, Mr Macintyre,

but there's literally nothing that I could do to help you.'

I was on my feet before they could stop me, thumbing the STOP switch and ripping out the spool. The mirror over the empty fireplace reflected a red-faced image, hair falling into its eyes. I shoved the trolley into the closet and kicked the door shut.

'Now you listen to me. You say you have no legal standing here. Well that's just great – it puts us on an even footing. I came to this office in good faith. You both knew what I was talking about after thirty seconds. You could have stopped me but you let me run on. Fuck you!'

Neither moved as I held my lighter to the tape and threw the blazing coil in the fireplace. I looked back from the hallway, my voice unsteady.

'And let me promise you this much, gentlemen. If I find trouble through anything you say or do I'll plaster the pair of you over every inch of space I can lay my hands on.'

I stood on the steps, knowing that I'd made a fool of myself but I was too hot to care. *These* were the swells Brown had in mind when he went over the wall, the Untouchables. If he'd ever reached this building he'd have lasted no more than the length of time it took Spitz to summon the law. I thought of calling Ilinka but there was a queue in the post office. I needed time and privacy. I walked slowly back towards the car. Duryea was waiting round the corner, wearing a sheepskin coat and a Basque beret. He must have left the office by another exit. He fell into step beside me, a different man now that he was on the street. His eyes were never still. He used the store windows as mirrors.

'Do you have a car?' he asked casually.

Commonsense told me that this wasn't a bust. There was nothing these people could *bust* me for.

'Under the trees,' I answered. There was nobody near the Peugeot. I unlocked and Duryea settled himself comfortably in the passenger-seat.

'O.K. Let's get down to business.'

It bugged me the way he lolled, arms spread over the seat, completely sure of himself. My voice was sour.

'What kind of business could we have together?'

There was a hint of condescension in his manner. 'Come off it, Mac. You're a newspaperman. You must know the way these things work. What happened back there was strictly for the record. This is for real.'

'It is, is it,' I said. 'Does that mean you intend to do something for the Browns?'

'First of all for you and for me,' he smiled. 'Understand me well. Everything Spitz said was true. The town dogcatcher has more standing in law here than we have. We couldn't arrest a five-legged poodle. What we're supposed to do is collect, collate and report back to Washington. And listen, of course. That's officially.'

The emblem on his tie-clip was a tiny gold parachute. 'How about unofficially?' I asked.

He juggled the question in his mind for a moment then closed an eye expressively.

'People come and go. We get around, Mac.'

'I'm impressed,' I said sarcastically.

His voice was mild. 'If we're going to work together, don't be so goddam spiky, feller. Look, we want a copy of Carnot's statement. And I'm going to help you get it.'

He unbuttoned the sheepskin coat then the Brooks Brothers jacket. I don't know whether it was intentional but the motions revealed a snub-nosed police-special in a holster under his left armpit.

'I'm not spiky, I'm careful,' I said. 'And I happen to be learning about a whole number of things. Have you got a permit for that gun?'

He grinned. 'Sure have. *That* they allow us. I'm still waiting for the sixty-four dollar question.'

I looked at him, baffled. 'Cue me in,' I suggested.

His grin widened. 'I'm a hungry office-boy looking for the better things in life. Washington's sitting on a barrel of information connected with these people you're chasing but it's scrambled. If you can get Carnot or someone to talk we're in business. I might even make promotion.' His eyes were very serious.

'I'll buy that,' I said. 'But there are quite a few people trying to climb aboard the bandwagon at the moment. Welcome. There's only one rule. We do things my way.'

He nodded. 'Sure thing, Mac. Whatever you say, anything at all. All I want is a peek at that statement. We'll even hold our report till you give us the word.' He put out his hand.

Over the past couple of days I seem to have been shaking hands like a campaigning senator. Duryea's grip was a good one.

'What else do you offer apart from the gun?' I demanded.

He flashed me his ace-in-the-hole grin. 'My mother was from Quebec. I speak fluent French and I do as I'm told. If that's not enough I've got a black Thunderbird with C.C. plates that are registered with the police. It helps in an emergency.'

A solitary pedestrian made his way down the path, his hands deep in his pockets. There was no cop nearer than thirty yards. I wound the window down and emptied the ash-tray.

'How much have you people got on Carnot?'

He shook his head decisively. 'Not a single thing. The name's a new one to us. Bernanos, Carnot – all new.'

I shut the window again. 'I'm going out to Carnot's house tonight.'

He narrowed his blue eyes. 'Well watch it. You just don't walk in on these guys and pound the table. You're out in the open, feller, with the lights full on you. There'll be other people there.'

'I doubt it,' I said. 'Carnot thinks I have Brown's envelope. The more he talks about it, the deeper the hole he digs for himself.'

He listened, his strong face thoughtful as I described Nagle's electronic equipment. The questions he put were technical and to the point. He told me that he'd taken a six weeks course with the F.B.I. in wire-tapping and allied activities.

'Let me see that belt,' he said suddenly. He inspected it thoroughly before returning it.

'I like that,' he announced. 'I've heard of them but this is the first I've seen. Where are you going to plant the receiver?'

I shrugged. 'Somewhere near Carnot's house. There's a range of a mile to play with.'

He wagged his forefinger. 'Too dangerous. Anything could happen. No, you use me as a backstop. I take the receiver. That way I'll know what's going on.'

I looked at him soberly. 'You could even make off with the tape.'

He nodded. 'That's right, too. But then you're sure that I won't. You want my honest opinion, Mac?'

'I collect them,' I said.

'Get rid of the other tapedeck, the dispatch-case or whatever. You can get too cute with guys like Carnot.'

I saw what he meant. The thought had already crossed my mind. 'You could be right at that,' I agreed. 'There's one thing I'd like you to do for me.'

He checked his watch. 'I have to get back to Spitz.'

'This is for later,' I said. 'I brought my secretary and a photographer over from London. They're one hundred per cent reliable. Could you pick them up at their hotels. We can all meet afterwards.'

His big jaw jutted. 'Not a chance. The deal's with you and no-one else. Sorry.'

'No sweat,' I shrugged. 'Then we'll meet at nine. Le Coq Hardi. It's a bistro opposite Notre Dame.'

He made a fist and rapped me on the arm with it lightly. 'Twenty-one hours and don't forget, dump that Dick Barton outfit. Don't even have it in your car.'

'Check,' I said. 'You realise that we'll only have one shot at the bastards, don't you?'

His smile came and went. 'How many do you need?'

I watched him across the street, the beret slouched on one side of his head, inconspicuous somehow despite the bulky sheepskin coat. I suddenly realised the significance of the emblem on his tie-clip. At some time he'd been a paratrooper. I drove down the Quai des Tuileries and forked right before reaching the underpass. There had been a thaw in the east and the Seine was an angry surge of grey water. I was making for a bar near the school of Beaux Arts. Jean-Paul Texier had been a painter before entering the movie-industry. We had spent an entire evening together, sitting around the places he'd frequented as a student. Some of them were pretty wild. The Q-Bar had changed hands since his time but it seemed the ideal place for me to make my phone-calls. I left the Peugeot on Rue Jacob and walked south, picking my way through the debris left by the street-traders. The Q-Bar was wedged between a couple of stores selling artists supplies. There was the usual sign 'Club Prive' which in France is no more than an excuse to throw you out if you don't look prosperous enough. I stepped into an atmosphere of Estee Lauder and yesterday's liquor. The bleached blonde I remembered vaguely was behind the bar buffing her nails. The place was, as I had hoped completely deserted. I nodded.

'Good-afternoon, Mademoiselle. I'd like a glass of scotch please, Teacher's.'

The blonde head was raised slowly, fingers lingering at the V of the taffeta blouse.

'Actually, dear, it's *Monsieur* – Patrick. I know your face. Are you someone famous?'

'Not recently,' I said. A look of puzzlement crept into his eyes. 'May I use your phone?' I added.

'Of course,' he said archly. 'No writing on the wall, please, dear.'

The door of the booth clicked shut blocking out every vestige of sound. The walls were covered with graffiti, most of them scatalogical. I called Misty and Tully and told them to meet me at eight. My last call was to the U.N.S.C.A.D. building. It took a long time to get through to the Director of Security. An uncompromising girl's voice asked me what I wanted. I told her.

'De la part de qui?' she snapped.

'Ross Macintyre,' I said distinctly.

There was an interlude of muffled voices and strange clicks. Then a man came on the line, his articulation clear and deliberate.

'Paul Carnot.'

'You recognise my name? You know who I am?'

'Yes.'

'Is it safe to talk?'

'Yes.'

I brought the telephone nearer my chin. 'You had my letter?' He said yes for the third time.

'Are you interested in my proposition?'

Caution crept into the well-bred voice. 'I think we should talk.'

'I'll be at your house at eleven tonight,' I replied. 'Twenty-three hours. No audience, remember. Just you and me.'

'Understood,' he agreed.

I wanted to leave him something to think about. I took a chance with Brown's hunch.

'We've identified the man with the limp,' I said and hung up. He hadn't sounded too worried but training could account for that. He was probably making plans for my reception at this very moment. The scotch was waiting on the bar. I drank it and pushed a bill at Patrick.

'If you get someone in here asking about me, the name is Smith.' I left him with his lips forming the name soundlessly.

The Citroens were lined against the convent wall like dark shiny roaches. Someone had broken off the icicles on the dolphins' mouths and water was dribbling into the basin below. Ilinka's drawing-room curtains were shut tight. I used the bell in the way she recognises. She let me in hurriedly. She was wearing a grey woollen dress fastened with a metal belt bearing the signs of the zodiac. I threw my coat at the chest in the hallway.

'Where are the others?'

She pointed upstairs. 'Watching television. They have reached the stage when they do not want to talk. I can understand it.'

I pulled her into the drawing-room and closed the door. The fire had the brightness that a cold day draws from beech-logs. The smell of the freesias mingled with that of wood-smoke. The flickering firelight behind drawn curtains made a refuge of the room. Ilinka sat on the sofa and pulled her legs up after her. I took a chair.

'O.K. Just how did you know that my calls from the Ritz were monitored?'

She looked at me slyly. 'Only *one* call, dear.'

'You're avoiding the question,' I said. *'How did you know?'*

She smiled brilliantly. There is no room as revealing as a bathroom and I know Ilinka's. She uses a tooth-paste that is scented with cinnamon and that stains the gums red. Ilinka is very aware of its aid to charm.

'I can never think properly when you are here. You are too restless. But after you left yesterday I remembered that you told me the police had taken note of some telephone numbers. So I made discreet inquiries.'

The television upstairs was playing the dated harmonies of the forties. I took a long deep breath.

'So which of the colonels was it this time?'

She smiled with an air of satisfaction, plumping the chintz curtains.

'Arrangements have to be made at the Centrale when an international call is monitored. Proper permission has to be given. The gentleman in charge of the mechanical process is a person called Plantin. The authority to monitor your call to London came from one of the S.D.E.C.E. bureaux.'

I brought my feet together and stared at them. 'So Mr Plantin knows my business?'

'Why not?' she challenged. 'Everyone else seems to know it.'

We glared at one another then her expression softened. 'You are big and brave, mon choux, but there are times when someone has to take you by the hand. Even if it is, how do you say – an old battleaxe like me.'

I grunted. Her little black book and the pearl-handled pistol were both out-of-sight.

'Has it ever occurred to you that *your* phone might be tapped?'

She waved the suggestion away blithely. 'Often. And sometimes it is. I always know beforehand. Please do not be cross with me, Ross, dear. I did not know what name you were using so I could not leave a message at Orly. But I did telephone your apartment in London. There was no reply.'

'There wouldn't be,' I said in a level voice. 'I wasn't there.'

'That much I gathered,' she observed drily. 'You brought Misty back with you.'

'And a photographer.'

She made a nest of her cushions and leaned back in it. 'What happens now?'

I told her my plan, pretty sure that she'd criticise it. But all she said was.

'I think you'd better tell the people upstairs.'

I called them down. Phoebe came first, her brother close behind her. They sat side-by-side. Ilinka patted the girl's knee.

'Ross has some good news for you.'

They turned their heads, their faces ruddy in the firelight. Their eyes had the intensity of spiritualists at a seance.

'We've achieved a lot,' I said. 'An agent from the United States Narcotics Bureau is working with us unofficially. If for any reason at all I don't show up here by tomorrow morning Ilinka will take you to the lawyer's office and you'll turn yourselves in. My secretary will be with you. She's got the entire story in her head. If the worst comes to the worst you have my word that my newspaper will print it. That in itself should get you off the hook.'

Phoebe swept the hair from her eyes. 'What does that mean, "if the worst comes to the worst"?'

'If I blow the scene with Carnot,' I said as nonchalantly as I could. 'I won't get a second crack at him.'

'But you *won't* blow it.' Brown's eyes were earnest behind his spectacles.

I turned to Ilinka. 'Susini claims that he has a judge in his pocket ready. A political buddy. Does that make sense?'

Her eyes slid to the fire and back. 'I would think so, yes. From what I've heard of Susini I would say it is likely. But if you succeeded with Carnot there will be a number of people anxious and able to help.'

She didn't have to tell me. I'd already made the point to Duryea. Once Carnot blew the whistle, there'd be a massed charge into the limelight, probably headed by Ilinka's colonels, sabres flashing. In the meantime the Union Corse would remove itself from the scene as neatly as a surgeon excises an appendix.

'Misty's coming here,' I told Ilinka. 'The photographer as well. You'll like Jim and it'll mean a man in the house.'

Brown blinked as his sister came to the rescue, hot-eyed with anger. 'That was an unnecessary thing to say!' she burst out.

I'd meant no offence. I wanted to tell her so, that the phrasing had been unfortunate. Ilinka stood up, took the cigarette from Phoebe's fingers and threw it into the fire. Her voice was sharp.

'This is no time for tantrums. Behave yourself.'

I looked over at Brown. 'Sorry.'

His hand came up as if it had weights attached. 'Forget it. I've never been described as a hero, anyway.'

Ilinka dominated us from the fireplace. 'Stuff and nonsense. It is not everyone who is able to meet danger unafraid. There are many forms of courage.'

'What are you looking at me for?' I asked defensively.

'Are you going to Carnot's house alone?' she demanded.

The convent bell tolled, the sound mournful. I came to my feet. 'That's the arrangement. The American won't be far away.'

Brown spoke in a low voice, looking into the fire, 'Whatever happens, Phoebe and I are deeply grateful to you.'

The expression in his sister's eyes told me that I was forgiven. 'He already knows that,' she said.

I opened the drawing-room door. 'So let's make sure there's something to be thankful *for*!'

Ilinka came out to the hallway with me. It could have been the lighting but her eyes were even more than usually brilliant. In anyone else I'd have suspected tears

but Ilinka never weeps. She lifted her face to be kissed.
'Don't you dare try to be a hero, Ross. Don't you dare!'

I pulled the door shut and heard the bolts rammed home. The lamps were burning in the square, the architects cars gone. The faint smell of a bonfire came from beyond the convent wall. I drove the Peugeot west as far as Boulevard Raspail. There's an hotel near the cemetery that has a Japanese-run sauna bath and an underground garage. It's always quiet there and the people leave you alone. I undressed in a cubicle, donned the white kimono and clogs and clumped through into a room where the dry heat smelled of eucalyptus trees. In twenty minutes the sweat was pouring from me. I lay naked on the wooden slats wondering what the hell I was doing with my life. In twenty years time I'd have to be very rich or very much loved. I couldn't see myself being either. The way things were going there was small hope of accomplishing more than I already had done. Misty and I were good for another couple of years at the most. Ilinka's judgement was sound enough. I had little to offer any woman and time would only make the lack more evident. My feeling was that it would probably be Misty who would make the final break. In a strange sort of way I was looking forward to it. There'd be nobody like her again, never. But what I'd be left with would be what I'd basically wanted, to go my own way with no responsibilities. I'd already made up my mind on the plane coming back that I'd make Baxter a present of the rest of my contract. I'd skip my bonus and leave on a high note. There was enough money in the bank for me to drop out of the sky on to an island where goats ate herbs and the sun warmed the rocks. I'd write the book

Ilinka always said I had in me, the book *I* knew I could write. It wasn't bad going for a kid from an orphanage.

I stretched out, tasting the salt on my lips. *The orphanage*. After all these years the memory was still there, defiantly recalled at times. The place had taught me one lesson at least, to make the best of what I had and was. I pressed the buzzer and a smiling Japanese girl with oiled black hair answered. Her strong hands eased the tension from my body. I asked her to call me at seven o'clock and stretched out on the floor, nothing beneath me but a raffia mat. I slept as I hadn't done in years, a dreamless suspension in time that left me completely refreshed. It was dark when the masseuse waked me, bowing and hissing through her teeth. I dressed slowly, putting everything out of my mind but the coming visit to Carnot. I was glad that I'd have Duryea near at hand. I *knew* I was no hero. Pig-headed if you like, obstinate but certainly not heroic. I paid my check and rode the elevator down to the basement.

There was a radio in the Peugeot. I switched it on and tried one station after another. L'Affaire Brown seemed to have dropped out of the news entirely. Baxter would be eating his fingers as the wire-reports piled up on his desk. No fresh snow had fallen in spite of the weather forecast and the streets were full of well-wrapped pedestrians. I took the Pont du Palais on to Ile-de-la-Cite. Left rose the sombre mass of the Palais-de-Justice. At the east end of the island the floodlit towers of Notre Dame soared, the stonework lavender and grey above the dark water. I drove past the barracks on to the short street where the flower-sellers stand during the day. I parked the Peugeot there and walked back past the gloom of Hotel Dieu. The red lamp that is Papa Stepka's own private joke glowed outside the bistro. I stepped into the appetising smell of onions frying. The room was empty except for Misty and Jim. The candles were lit and clean glasses sparkled on freshly-ironed tablecloths. Madame Stepka poked her head out of the serving-area, withdrawing it when she recognised me. I sat with the others.

'Anything happen?'

Tully was drinking beer. There was a bottle of Perrier in front of Misty. She was wearing the velvet cap on the back of her head. She cupped her chin in a hand, the band of freckles wrinkling across her nose.

'There's a New Testament in my room,' she announced. 'It's in French but it's printed in Hong Kong.'

She was obviously nervous but come to that so was I. 'Very significant,' I kidded.

Tully closed an eye. 'I love this chick. Her mind's always on the higher things.' His bony shoulders poked through his trenchcoat. A hot Queensland sun has burned every ounce of excess fat from his body.

'I can guess what's coming,' Misty said bleakly. 'While you two blades ramble round I'm going to be left having a cosy tete-a-tete with Mme Ostrava.'

I shook my head again. 'Wrong. Jim's going with you.'

Tully's grin was amiable. 'It suits me, mate. As long as the old broad's got some beer.'

'She doesn't drink beer,' I replied. 'And you can mind your language and spare her the Fabian lectures. They wouldn't be appreciated.'

He made a face at Misty. 'Watch it. Come the revolution they're going to hang this joker from a lamp-post.'

'You got it wrong,' I smiled. 'Come the revolution,

you and your buddies will be in a concentration-camp.' I reached across the table and took Misty's hand. 'Smile for me, I coaxed.

She pulled her hand away, opened her purse and pulled out a mirror. She averted her mouth when I tried to kiss her. You're supposed to surrender when she's in this sort of mood. I wasn't going to.

I shrugged at Tully. 'She knows the address. Take a cab. Once you're inside the house, you open the door to nobody, got it. Police, firemen, *nobody*!'

He lounged to his feet, touching Misty's shoulder. 'Come on, mate, we're no longer wanted.'

She tucked her arm through his and sailed through the door without looking back. I watched them through a chink in the curtains till they turned the corner. Duryea arrived on the dot. The bistro had filled by now and it was a while before he located me. I ordered a couple of peppered steaks.

'O.K.,' I said, once Mme Stepka had gone. 'There's something on your mind, let's have it.'

He ran his fingers through his pine-dust hair. 'It's Spitz. He's getting cold feet. If you flunk this one, we never heard of you.'

I took a deep drag on the butt in my fingers. 'That didn't take too much figuring. I don't aim to flunk.'

He nodded, half to me, half to himself. 'Then Spitz'll love you, baby. We both will.'

The food was served and we ate in silence. I didn't enjoy the meal for some reason and the beer tasted flat. Duryea blocked an incipient belch and searched his pockets for a pack of BISODOL tablets.

'What's the programme?'

I leaned forward, my elbows dragging the tablecloth.

'There's this hotel on Boulevard Raspail called the Alliance. It has a garage underneath. The moment you see me leave Carnot's place, make for the garage and wait there for me. I drive in, switch to your car and we drive out again. That way if there's anyone on our tail, we'll lose them.'

'You'll do,' he said. 'The Alliance, right. Now I've checked the street-map of Versailles. Carnot's house is near the municipal swimming-baths. They're out of doors and closed till May. There's plenty of cover there and several ways of working back to Carnot's place. I'll park there. Did you dump the big recorder?'

I pointed at it over by the wall. 'The Stepkas will take care of it for me. We'd better make a move.'

He stuck his beret on his head and I followed him out to the Thunderbird. He'd left it slap-bang outside the headquarters of the Police Judiciaire on Quai des Orfevres. We sat in it while he examined the camouflaged razor-set.

'O.K.,' he nodded. 'We'll try it out. Up and down the street once and keep talking.'

The few people I met gave me the kind of look people reserve for idiots. I kept going, making for the point of the island and talking to myself. The two streams of the river joined in an angry torrent that surged towards the Pont des Arts. I gave it a couple of minutes, switched off the mike and hurried back to the Thunderbird. Duryea held up his thumb, grinning.

'You got yourself a good piece of equipment here. There's some background noise but the man spoke the truth. I was getting you loud and clear.' He returned the reel to the start position, closed the case and put it on the seat beside him. 'What's with the poetry, anyway?'

The car was full of the smell of his indigestion tablets. 'The poetry. Well, that's the Burial of Sir John Moore at Coruna. I had to learn it as a kid. The bit about "the sods with their bayonets turning" always used to get me. I've never forgotten it.'

He opened the glove compartment. I could see the revolver inside, a match for his own. His voice was offhand.

'You want it, you're welcome.'

There was this Pistol-and-Rifle club I'd belonged to in Montreal. I'd go there Sunday mornings, playing the part of the Intrepid Reporter blasting his way off the Bucharest Express. It got to be so that I could finally hit a barn-door provided that I was standing close enough. I left the gun where it was. He shrugged and pushed the flap up again.

'Suit yourself. How do we go?'

'Porte Maillot, the Bois de Boulogne then out on to the auto-route. I'm parked behind the Conciergerie. Give me a couple of minutes to get back.'

In spite of the bitter weather the hookers' cars were parked under the lights along the Allee de Longchamps. Frozen water glimmered beyond the expanses of grass. We increased speed once on the auto-route, employing the leap-frog technique. I'd lead for a while then Duryea would take over. The manoeuvre minimised the chance that we were being followed. Versailles is a dead place in winter, remembered for wind rattling torn posters on the bill-boards, crocodile-lines of disconsolate schoolgirls kicking through fallen leaves. Duryea roared past, indicating that he was going to make a left turn. I followed the Thunderbird down an avenue lined with chestnut trees. His trafficator was going again, pointing out Carnot's house. It was a Charles Addams building with steep slate roofs and pointed gables. A hanging lamp illuminated the front door, more lights were burning downstairs. The Thunderbird turned right on to a gravel-topped lane and stopped in front of some chained turnstiles. Weathered posters advertised last season's attractions. Someone had put a rock through the window of the phone booth. We both cut our lights. I walked across to the other car.

'How did it look to you?'

I could see the tape-recorder on the seat beside him. 'Pretty good,' he said.

I gave the belt-buckle a quarter-turn. 'Well, here goes.'

'Yeah, take it easy.'

'You, too,' I said. I circled the block coming back on to the avenue from the far end. The light over the front door went out as I turned the Peugeot on to the driveway. A clump of spindly evergreens and some dank laurel grew close to the wall. I could see the rear end of a car parked in the coachyard. I stood in the cold still air like a man on the edge of a silent forest wishing that he'd brought his high boots. I heard a watercloset being flushed inside the house, a cough. Two steps led up to the varnished mahogany door. It opened as my fingers found the bell-push.

I'd built up a mental picture of Carnot over the last few days. A tall man, balding and fiftyish with a scythe of mouth and probing eyes. The guy in front of me was no more than a couple of years older than me and dressed in a well-tailored grey suit. His face was deeply tanned, his black hair bisected by a slash of white. He opened the door wider, glancing outside before he shut it again.

I cleared the length of my throat. 'Carnot?'

He turned the key in the lock. 'Carnot was unable to keep the appointment. I am his deputy.'

He led the way into a room furnished as a study. The deep shelves were stacked with books. English fox-hunting prints hung on the walls and there was a bronze horse on the desk. His accent still puzzled my ear. It was almost like an Italian speaking French. And suddenly I knew who he was. The name was out of my mouth before I could think.

'You're Pelazzi!'

He stared at me with the eyes of a cat. 'My compliments. You obviously have good sources of information.'

The streak of white ran from just above his forehead to the crown of his head, the width of a chisel-blade. It was as if his hair had been parted with an axe at some time and grown back in another colour. He moved lightly and when he came to a stop he was very still. We sat down in front of the fire. I kept thinking of Duryea, recording every sound in the room, the tick of the clock, the creak of the leather under me. I lit a cigarette.

'My deal was with Carnot. Nobody else.'

He leaned back, clasping a knee in the pose favoured by photographers. 'Let me put your mind at rest. Carnot and I are very close. We have no secrets from one another. I understand that you have something to sell, is that right?'

Footsteps crossed the hallway, slow and deliberate. If this was a war of nerves, they weren't doing badly.

'That's right.'

He smiled. 'I have the general idea. But I'd like some details.'

I watched the smoke trickle through my fingers then looked up. 'We have a detailed record of all the heroin processed by Juan Bernanos. Delivery-dates, particulars of the amounts and the Polaroid prints, of course.'

'Of course,' he agreed. 'The man with the limp.' His smile was brilliant.

'The package is yours for half-a-million dollars,' I said.

He moved from his chair and sat behind the desk. 'You're supposed to be a reporter, is that correct?'

I tried for easy confidence. 'I *am* a reporter. But I don't intend to stay one for much longer.'

Pelazzi lifted the bronze horse, weighing it in his palm as he looked down the length of the room. The white door at the end was shut.

'Of course not, with half-a-million dollars. What makes you think that Carnot has this sort of money?'

I shook my head. 'I wasn't thinking of Carnot. I was thinking of the people behind him.'

He was tracing with his finger on the blotter, his head cocked sideways.

'And what happens if you don't make your sale?'

'We've thought of that,' I parried. 'There's another potential buyer – someone with political ambitions.' I was showing the stamp of a classy liar, believing what I said.

The expression on his face told me that at least I had scored one hit.

'Is the idea of extortion yours or Brown's?'

I waved my cigarette. 'Initially his. I am responsible for the refinements.'

He put both elbows on the desk, looking at me curiously. 'Were you ever in jail? Have you mixed with thieves?'

'Neither.' I'd no idea what he was getting at.

He gave a sort of explanation. 'I was wondering about your loyalty to Brown. Why don't you and I do a deal and forget about him?'

'Brown has the envelope,' I answered. 'He always has had it.'

His movement was so swift that the gun was welded to his hand before I realised what was happening. It was an automatic fitted with a silencer and the barrel was level with my chest.

Pelazzi's voice was curt. 'On your feet.' He searched me thoroughly, touching the belt-buckle at least three times. Then he pursed his lips and spat full in my face. He shoved me down the room to the white-painted door. 'Turn the handle,' he ordered.

I wiped his spittle from my cheek and obeyed. The dining-room table was set for two people, one at each end. Leaning with their backs against the wall were the two cops who had come to Gunn's. A slightly-built man in a brown tweed suit was sitting on a chair betwen them. His hair was damp with sweat.

'This is your visitor, Paul,' said Pelazzi. 'I want you to take a good look at him and tell me if you have seen him before.'

Carnot's head lifted slowly, his eyes terrified. One of the cops coughed.

'Think!' urged Pelazzi, smiling encouragingly. 'At a press-conference, perhaps?'

Carnot licked his lips, relief flooding back into his face. 'No. No, Pierre. I never saw this man before, I am sure of it.'

I watched powerless as Pelazzi moved behind, bringing the gun up close to Carnot's head.

'Adieu, Paul,' said Pelazzi then the gun jumped in his hand.

The top of Carnot's head literally lifted, blood, bone and brain mushrooming out of a gaping hole. He slumped forward, hitting the floor hard as he fell. The two cops stepped away, their faces expressionless. The air was pungent with burnt cordite and my ears still rang with the noise of the explosion. Gas leaked from the silence as Pelazzi raised the gun. His face conveyed the contempt that a professional killer has for an extortioner.

'Crapaud,' he snarled. 'Scum!'

My mind was assembling the pieces, slowly and painfully. I'd just been chopped off at the knees, tricked. Carnot's death broke the last direct link with the Union Corse. It made Brown's envelope worthless. Whoever it was in the Polaroid prints would be like Carnot, expendable. All that remained now was the wrap-up – the bullet here and there closing those few mouths that might produce a whisper. And mine would be first. I choked back the bile in my throat, trying to remember a prayer. *Surely by now Duryea was doing something!*

Pelazzi propped himself against the edge of the table. His shoe was touching Carnot's leg but he seemed unaware of it.

'Now you and I will talk business,' he said. 'I offer you your own life in exchange for Brown's. You have ten seconds to make up your mind.' He consulted the watch on his wrist. 'Five!'

There's a great deal of wishful thinking about the

roles we play in time of danger. We see ourselves wrapped in the flag defying death to save the lives of others. If Misty or Ilinka had been in the room at that moment I hope I'd have taken a bullet that was meant for either. But they were fifteen miles away and by now Duryea would surely have alerted the authorities. He had Ilinka's phone-number and address.

The gun lifted. 'Where is Brown?' asked Pelazzi.

All three men were watching me closely. There was no question of me leading them on a false trail. The first wrong move would send me to join Carnot.

'In a house in the Fifth Arondissement,' I said. 'Place des Religieuses.'

The pupils of Pelazzi's eyes contracted. He pulled a cheap string of rosary beads from his pocket and dropped them on Carnot's chest. The dead man's face was a welter of blood. His denture was halfway through his open mouth. Pelazzi stepped over the body.

'Allez!'

They herded me into a Mercedes 280, the two cops sitting up front, Pelazzi beside me. It was difficult to believe that he had just blown a hole in someone's head. His face was thoughtful as he ordered the dash lights to be extinguished. I wedged myself in the corner, as far away from him as I could. We passed the cut-off leading to the swimming-pool. A bend in the road prevented me from seeing if the Thunderbird was still there. Even if Duryea had been in Carnot's garden there'd been time for him to double back and use the phone outside the baths. Now every yard we covered was taking me out of his range. The cop at the wheel drove with speed and certainty as if repeating a trip made many times before. Occasionally he'd let a word drift back, a comment on the traffic or the route he was taking. Lights and houses flicked by. There were no barricades across the road, no flashing lamps, no sign that the hunt was on for the big black car. Signals held us at the Pont D'Iena. I could see the faces in the car beside us, a man and a woman, relaxed and incurious. The door-catch was close to my fingers.

Pelazzi moved his head, his voice disdainful. 'You'd never make it.'

Minutes later, the Mercedes whispered across Place Monge into the narrow streets. My voice was working badly.

'Make a left and then a right.'

The driver killed the motor in front of the convent wall. Pelazzi scanned the scene, his nose thin with caution. The only light other than the street-lamp came from Ilinka's house.

'Is that it?' he asked. I nodded. The quiet in the square was unnatural. I could hear the water dripping a dozen feet away.

'Take a look,' ordered Pelazzi. The cop at the wheel unfastened his door. He moved round the square, a shadow among the shadows, avoiding Ilinka's lighted window. He came back and nodded. Pelazzi nudged me out of the car. I crossed the square knowing that the two people who mattered most in life to me were behind those drawn curtains, waiting for my return. The only thing that stuck in my mind was that Tully wouldn't open the door. Pelazzi's gun was hard against my back. He indicated the bell-push. I pressed it. The chimes rang in the kitchen. Nobody answered. Pelazzi stabbed the button hard. The summons remained unanswered, the house completely silent. Pelazzi stepped sideways and shattered the drawing-room window with his gun.

The flat-eared cop hauled himself through the curtains, taking the centre part of the frame with him. The street door opened. A shove sent me into the hallway. Pelazzi pinned me against the wall as one of the cops tore upstairs, the other into the study. The flat-eared cop leaned over the banisters, his hat and cot coat spangled with fragments of broken glass. He shook his head. His partner appeared in the drawing-room doorway.

'Nobody!'

Pelazzi's eyes levelled on me. I knew what he was thinking, that I'd somehow warned Brown. There's a myth about waiting for death with your life flashing through your brain like a speeded-up film. It's not true. It's the future you're concerned with and not the past.

Pelazzi stepped away from the wall, indicating the door with his gun-hand.

'Wait a minute! You pulled the bolts before you let us in. He is still in the house. Look again.'

The drawing-room curtains rattled along the rail. Something heavy toppled over up in Ilinka's bedroom. Pelazzi's eyes wavered momentarily. I hurled myself through the kitchen door, jammed the table against the handle and tore down the garden path. The ivy over the iron door in the wall had been torn aside. Shouts came from the house. I could see the cop in Ilinka's bedroom struggling to open the window. I put my shoulder against the door. It didn't budge, locked on the other side. I jumped at the nearest tree, swinging from the branch and then clawing my way up, using heels, knees and hands. A ladder of branches took me to one that was parallel with the top of the convent wall. There was no time to think, only to jump. I hit the top of the wall like a man jumping into a saddle, thighs and wrists taking most of the shock. A bullet whined past as I flattened myself on the brickwork. I let myself hang at arm's length and then dropped. I picked myself out of the dead bonfire and ran towards the lighted windows of the chapel. A glimmer of concrete walk threaded the iron-hard grass. Somebody rattled the door in the wall. I stopped as everything went quiet. There was a complete hush as an unseen conductor lifted his baton and then lights flooded the sky, silhouetting the roof of Ilinka's house. A voice came from the direction of the square.

'Police! Surrender yourselves! We have the whole area surrounded!'

Car-horns blared from all points of the compass, confirming the warning. The beam of the searchlight travelled slowly over the rooftops. The three men clinging to the top of the convent wall were invisible to anyone on the square. I moved as the first man dropped. My fists pounded on a door in the main convent building.

'Open up, Jim!' I shouted. 'For Chrissakes open up! Tully, it's me!'

The cop was on the bull-horn again. 'We know you're in there, Pelazzi. Come out with your hands up!'

The door shuddered under the force of my blows. I ducked as the first cop reached me, avoiding the first karate chop. Then my neck was locked in the crook of the man's elbow. My brain, deprived of blood, seemed to bulge through my eye-sockets. Pelazzi fired at the door. The lock sagged in a framework of splintered wood. The weight of two men was hurled against it and we stumbled into a cold arched hall. A group of nuns was standing in front of a plaster statue of the Holy Family, each trying to hide behind the other. The cop released the pressure on my jugular and my mind started to function again. There was only one light, high in the ceiling. But it was enough to recognise the nun in the white wimple. It was Ilinka, her body draped in her friend's habit. The chapel door was open at the end of the corridor. I could see the pews full of kneeling nuns. There was no sign of Misty, Tully or the Browns.

The entrance-doors were immediately in front of us. Wheels clipped the edge of the pavement as the hunt located us. One of the cops had lost his hat and Pelazzi's overcoat was ripped in two places. He fished some loose shells from his pocket and reloaded the gun. His tanned face was sweating.

'Over here, Reverend Mother.' His voice was firm but respectful.

I looked at her as I would at a stranger. Her face had the serenity of the woman's whose role she had taken.

'This is the house of God, my son,' she said in a level voice.

Pelazzi nodded, his eyes everywhere. 'It's too late to worry about that, Reverend Mother. You are a hostage and I have no wish to be forced to pray for your soul's repose.'

His free hand was gripping my arm just above the elbow. The bull-horn roared in the street, directly outside.

'It's Commissaire Kerroux – you know me, Pelazzi. Give yourself up. I promise you fair treatment.'

The nuns in the entrance-hall were as still as the statue behind them. A chanting started in the chapel as someone led the congregation in prayer. The beam of a powerful searchlight filtered through the cracks in the door. Pelazzi watched it carefully, the hand holding his gun completely steady. A wounded leopard would have surrendered more readily.

My voice was cracked and unsteady. 'Let me talk to the police. We can make a deal.'

He pushed Ilinka and me forward, shielding himself behind us as the flat-eared cop threw the door open. Pelazzi put the gun to Ilinka's head, shouting into the glare of the searchlight.

'These people are coming with me, Kerroux. Their lives are in your hands. Clear the neighbourhood and leave one car out front with the motor running!'

The cop shut the door again, pressing himself against the wall so that he could see through the window at the street. The entrance-hall darkened as the searchlight was extinguished. The chanting from the chapel gained volume . . . blessed art Thou among women . . . The cop at the window turned.

'They're going.'

Pelazzi cocked his head, listening intently. Ilinka was standing meekly, arms folded in her sleeves. The cops voice came hoarse and triumphant.

'They've left the car. The street's clear.'

'Open the doors,' Pelazzi ordered. 'Check the car. You take the cemetery, Salvatore.'

A low parapet enclosed the small graveyard opposite. The high garden wall afforded no cover on the convent side of the street. The yellow headlamps of the parked police-car stared out into the night. The two cops ran down the steps, fanning out with their guns in their hands. One circled the car, checked the interior and looked underneath. He held up his thumb. His partner was out-of-sight behind a vault. Pelazzi motioned us down the steps. Ilinka came slowly, old suddenly and frail, her habit brushing the ground. My move to help her was involuntary. Pelazzi knocked my arm up and the barrel of his gun dug into my kidney.

'Look after yourself,' he snarled.

We were no more than a foot in front of her when a pistol roared almost deafening me. Pelazzi lurched forward, mouth opening in a noiseless cry. A look of surprise spread over his face and blood gushed from his open mouth. He fell heavily. The pearl-handled pistol Ilinka had been hiding in her sleeve fell to the ground. Footsteps pounded across the graveyard. I grabbed Ilinka, pulled her down in my arms and rolled with her towards the gutter. A shot cracked from the darkness. The man by the police-car staggered then righted himself and took careful aim, holding the gun with both hands. Something smashed into my left shoulder with the impact of a mule-kick. I was vaguely conscious of people running, of lights and voices. Then nothing.

I opened my eyes in an unfamiliar room. A spider crouched on the whitewash immediately overhead. There was a crucifix on the wall, an iron-stand with an enamelled bowl where a bearded man was washing his hands. The bed moved and Misty's hand touched my face. It was agony to move. My left shoulder was heavily strapped. It felt as if the same mule had kicked me half a dozen times in rapid succession. Misty's eye makeup had streaked but her eyes were jubilant. My vision focused gradually, taking in the rest of the scene. The doorway was crowded with people. Ilinka was sitting on a chair, still dressed in the Mother Superior's robes. I could see the Browns, Duryea and Susini. Tully was outside in the corridor talking to a man in uniform. The bearded man clapped his hands.

'Bon, Messieurs, Mesdames. The spectacle is over. As

you can see the patient is very much alive.'

He groped in a leather bag, fitted a phial to a needle and squirted a trial jet of liquid into the air. The smell of disinfectant, the sight of the blood-stained rags in the basket, made me feel like throwing up. The doctor found a vein in the crook of my right elbow. It swelled under the pressure of his thumb. He dabbed it with a ball of cotton. His breath smelled of cloves.

'This will make you sleep. Don't worry about the proprieties. Reverend Mother has a dispensation from the Bishop.'

I looked across the room, thoughts scrambling. Ilinka's eyes were very wise. I tried to heave myself up, to ask a hundred questions, but a depth of shimmering water had somehow washed between us. Faces spread and lengthened like images in a carnival mirror. Susini's voice came from a great distance. The words were unintelligible but it didn't matter. Ilinka's eyes had given me my answer. I let myself slip into the water, holding on tight to Misty's hand.

POSTSCRIPT

I had what could be called a working honeymoon. I wrote the book in five months, sitting under a banana-palm while Misty rolled in the surf. Her own version is that she was in the house doing my typing. Anyway, the publishers sent me two sets of galleys. I sent one to George Gunn. It was six weeks before I had an answer. The letter was written from Paris.

Gunn's Hotel.
Place des Vosges
4e.

Hi, Ross:

I read your book. About this thing of me suing you for libel and making your goddam fortune absolutely not. You'd probably make most of that stuff stick anyway. You always were a brazen-faced liar.

I saw the newsreel where you got married. All that capering and grinning put me off my food. Anyone would think you invented the whole business. The girl has my sympathy.

The book wasn't that bad. I read all the bits about me three times so that I remember to boot your butt the next time we meet. I kept thinking about that letter – the letter that started it all. There'd been a five-day trial, all those witnesses and not a goddam one of you seemed to know what had happened to Bernanos' envelope.

So finally I had an idea. You owe me forty-seven dollars, Canadian, for a mixed bunch of roses, two bottles of champagne and a long weepy evening. That's right, with Hendrikson's chick. She's still working at the travel-agency, still loves the guy and, you're damned right, remembers that letter. Come to think of it, she's the only person who would. Now get this. The envelope turned up in Paris just eleven days ago, redirected from San Francisco by way of London, Berlin. Manila and Hong Kong. She said there were more finger-marks on it than a boy-burglar leaves on a street-door.

You know what she did with it? She sent it to the Dead Letter Office. So there's the end to your story. I hope it makes your day out there in Semolina. Don't try coming back to France for a while. Somebody might do you an injury.

And remember what Constable Sawchuk used to tell us. It's as easy to travel first-class as third. All you need is the money.

Best to you both,
George.

›› If you've enjoyed this book and would like to discover more great vintage crime and thriller titles, as well as the most exciting crime and thriller authors writing today, visit: ›››

The Murder Room

Where Criminal Minds Meet

themurderroom.com

www.ingramcontent.com/pod-product-compliance
Ingram Content Group UK Ltd.
Pitfield, Milton Keynes, MK11 3LW, UK
UKHW022312280225
455674UK00004B/276